"I know of a job vacancy that might suit you."

She opened her eyes and turned her head, still nestled on the leather headrest, to face him, not bothering to hide her suspicion. "You suddenly became Santa Claus?"

"No, I suddenly became in need of a wife."

She struggled to match Sebastian's flippancy. "Is that a proposal?"

"Yes."

The color flared hot and then faded pale in her cheeks as she sat bolt upright and reached for the door handle. "I'm assuming this is some sort of joke. Word to the wise—don't give up your day job. Stand-up is *not* your thing."

"What I am suggesting is a business arrangement." Only his long fingers silently drumming on the steering wheel suggested he was not as relaxed as he appeared.

Mari's fingers tightened on the door handle. "Hate is not a good basis for a business arrangement."

"I've factored that in," he retorted with unimpaired cool. "In public we would act the happy, loved-up couple."

A hissing sound left her lips. "Marriage. You're *actually* talking about *marriage*—it's not a sick joke?"

Seven Sexy Sins

The *true* taste of temptation!

From greed to gluttony, lust to envy, these
fabulous stories explore what seven sexy sins
mean in the twenty-first century!

Whether pride goes before a fall,
or wrath leads to passion that consumes entirely,
one thing is certain...the road to true love
has never been more enticing!

So you decide:

How can it be a sin when it feels so good?

Sloth—Cathy Williams

Lust—Dani Collins

Pride—Kim Lawrence

Gluttony—Maggie Cox

Greed—Sara Craven

Wrath—Maya Blake

Envy—Annie West

Seven titles by some of Harlequin Presents®
most treasured and exciting authors!

Kim Lawrence

—

The Sins of Sebastian Rey-Defoe

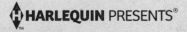

HARLEQUIN PRESENTS®

ISBN-13: 978-0-373-13815-9

The Sins of Sebastian Rey-Defoe

First North American Publication 2015

Copyright © 2015 by Kim Lawrence

Recycling programs for this product may not exist in your area.

This edition published by arrangement with Harlequin Books S.A.

For questions and comments about the quality of this book, please contact us at CustomerService@Harlequin.com.

Printed in U.S.A.

www.Harlequin.com

Kim Lawrence lives on a farm in Anglesey with her university lecturer husband, assorted pets who arrived as strays and never left, and sometimes one or both of her boomerang sons. When she's not writing, she loves to be outdoors, gardening or walking on one of the beaches that the island is famous for—along with being the place where Prince William and Catherine made their first home!

Books by Kim Lawrence

Harlequin Presents

One Night with Morelli
Captivated by Her Innocence
The Petrelli Heir
Santiago's Command
Stranded, Seduced...Pregnant
Unworldly Secretary, Untamed Greek
Under the Spaniard's Lock and Key
The Sheikh's Impatient Virgin

Royal & Ruthless
The Heartbreaker Prince

One Night With Consequences
A Secret Until Now

At His Service
Maid for Montero

Protecting His Legacy
Gianni's Pride

Visit the Author Profile page at Harlequin.com for more titles.

Thanks Peter

PROLOGUE

Blaisdon Gazette. 17 November 1990

> *A hospital spokesman this morning said that two babies, believed to be twins, found yesterday on the steps of St Benedict's Church, are now in a serious but stable condition. Police are anxious to trace the mother, who might be in need of medical care.*

London Reporter. 17 November 1990

> *The foundation stone of the hospital's new wing was laid by the late Sebastian Rey's grandson, who was named after his philanthropist grandfather. Stepping in for his father, whose duties captaining the Argentine national polo team kept him away from the ceremony, seven-year-old Sebastian Rey-Defoe is the son of the well-known English socialite Lady Sylvia Defoe. Sebastian is set to inherit the Rey billions and the Man-*

deville Hall estate in England. He suffered only minor injuries in the crash that killed his grandfather outright.

14 February 2008

'THERE IS A REASON, I suppose, why I am staying in a place called the Pink Unicorn?' Not a name you could say and think of minimalist decor, and not a name Seb could even say without a grimace of distaste.

'Sorry.' His irritatingly cheerful PA pretended she hadn't heard the sarcasm. 'But it is Valentine's Day and there isn't a decent place within twenty miles of Fleur's school that isn't fully booked. The Lake District is considered romantic. Don't worry, it's not contagious,' she soothed. 'And it is five star, so you won't be slumming it, and it has great reviews—people on the website rave about the little personal touches. Your room is… What does it say…? That was it: charming and bijou with beams and—'

'Oh, God!' he groaned. Six-five in his bare feet, he did not do bijou or beams… Was his petite PA punishing him for something?

'Don't be such a misery. You're very lucky that the Pink Unicorn had a cancellation.'

'I've sacked people for less. I'm ruthless, haven't you heard?' The previous month's article in a particular Sunday supplement, even though it had spawned several rebuttal articles in well-known financial journals, had left a public perception of him that suggested his wealth could not have been made without an utterly ruthless disregard for the rules or his fellow man.

'Where would you find someone else who gets your weird sense of humour?'

'You think I'm joking?'

'Or someone who is as efficient as me who doesn't weep when you scowl or fall in love with you when you don't?'

He fought back a smile and, with resignation in his voice, grumbled, 'Who the hell calls a place the Pink Unicorn?'

Now Seb knew—the same people who sat a poor guy with a classical guitar out on a lawn on a zero-degree February evening that neither the heat from a glowing brazier nor the open-sided gazebo affair lit by lanterns offered any protection against. To add insult to injury they'd had him wear some ridiculous Spanish get-up that no real Spaniard would have been seen dead in, while he played a cheesy love song in the candlelight as loved-up couples groped one another.

Sebastian's lip curled. If this was romance, they could keep it!

It was a spectacularly stomach-churning sight,

but probably a fitting end, he mused, to a day where the high point had been getting a parking fine from an overzealous attendant.

It *should* have been a good day, a celebratory occasion. His thirteen-year-old half-sister had won the under-fifteens prize at the science fair her school was hosting, and against all the odds their mother, Lady Sylvia Defoe, had turned up in a display of rare parental support.

He should have known better, yet, as she had walked into the room causing conversations to stop, taking the attention as her due, Seb had almost got sucked in by the 'caring mother' act.

Until, that was, she had stepped back from the arm's-length maternal embrace, looked at her daughter's face and delivered some very loud advice on skin care, adding complacently that *she* had never had acne or actually even a spot, and then, presumably because she had not traumatised her thirteen-year-old daughter enough, she had gone on to flirt with every male in the room that caught her eye while her daughter had cringed and wished herself elsewhere. Seb, who had been there, done that, had felt his half-sister's pain as his own anger had built.

The breaking point had come when Seb had found their mother in a classroom in a *very* close embrace with the newly married biology teacher. The doors had been wide open—anyone could have seen—but then maybe that was the idea. His mother loved nothing better than creating a scene.

Offering the embarrassed man a tissue for the lipstick smeared across his red face, he'd then suggested the teacher might like to rejoin his wife. Seb had waited until the teacher had gratefully scuttled away before asking his mother, on whom subtlety was wasted, point-blank what the hell she thought she was doing.

'I don't know why you're cross, Seb?' She'd pouted. 'Why *shouldn't I* have a bit of fun? *Your* father had an affair with that awful...' She'd given a heartbroken sob and allowed the tears she could produce at will to fall.

'I've heard it all before, Mother, so don't expect any sympathy from me. Get divorced, have affairs, get remarried—I'm bored with the entire never-ending cycle—but if you embarrass Fleur again, we're finished.'

The tears had stopped; she'd actually looked almost scared. Even though he'd known it wouldn't last, it had still made him feel like a bastard.

'You don't mean that, Seb.'

On the point of retracting, he'd pulled back. 'Every word,' he had lied. No matter what she did, she would always be his mother, but this was about Fleur, and she needed protecting.

'Do you ever think about the people you hurt when you're doing exactly what you want?' He'd searched her beautiful face for a moment before shaking his head. 'Sorry, that was a stupid question.'

A scowl glued to a face that caused several female heads to turn his way, Seb strode towards the entrance of the Pink Unicorn that had been geared out for the occasion with, surprise, surprise, garlands of dried red roses. If there was one of those damn things on his pillow he would... He sighed and thought, what was the point? The rest of the world was so caught up with the romance fable one single voice of logic would be lost in the brainless babble.

Allowing himself a superior smile, he turned his head to brush the snowflakes that had begun to fall off his shoulder. The night might end with a few cases of exposure, he thought as his cynical stare brushed over the heads of the clusters of couples. The mild contempt etched into his lean patrician features gave way to one of stark shock as his sweeping survey came to a shuddering stop.

As he stared, the scorch of heat that began in his belly spread through his body like flash fire, darkened the intense brown of his deepset eyes, framed by straight, strongly delineated brows almost as dark as his long, curling lashes, to jet black.

He didn't notice what she was wearing beyond the fact the dress she had on was blue and he would very much have liked to see her without it. She had a sensational body, sinuous curves and endless legs, and the lust that had erupted at the sight of her gave a fresh kick in his belly and lower, where it settled as his hot, hungry stare slid over those delectable curves before he dragged it back to her face.

The sense of recognition was crazy because he had never even imagined a woman who looked like her, let alone met one. Her face was a perfect oval, but it was not the symmetry of her features that held his gaze or caused his stomach muscles to clench viciously, but her expression, as, laughing, she looked up at the falling snow, her head thrown back a little to reveal the long, graceful curve of her throat.

Her lips were full, her eyes big in the light from an overhead lantern, her hair a wild explosion of tempestuous colour, gold, red, then gold again, curls that fell down her slender back almost to her waist.

A whoosh of cold air hit his face, breaking the grip of the spell that had held him motionless for countless seconds. Lowering his heavy eyelids long enough to give his nervous system time to recover from the carnal impact of the redhead, Seb dragged a hand across his dark hair and released the breath that had been trapped in his chest in a long, slow, hissing sigh.

He looked again, already distancing himself from that initial uncontrollable *visceral* reaction. It had been a long day and he'd been too long *without*… There are some things, thought Seb, that a man cannot rely on his PA to schedule… *Like a life*…?

Just as he was making a mental note to free up his weekend and deciding who he might share it with—that part had never been hard for him— the redhead's laughter drifted his way. Low and husky, it had a deliciously *tactile* quality. It felt like a finger running up and down his spine.

Not accustomed to envy, he experienced a twinge of something close to that emotion as he turned his critical, hostile gaze on the man who had invited this laughter…husband…lover…? As the thought slid through Seb's head the man in question turned and placed a hand under his partner's chin, drawing her face up to his.

This time, the sense of recognition Seb experienced was not to be wondered at: the lucky man was the husband of the local GP. Alice Drummond was a woman Seb had time for. She juggled a demanding career with two children and a husband who, at twenty, had written one book someone had called insightful, which was the sum total of his achievements to date, and he was still living off the kudos.

When he wasn't having romantic weekends with redheads with endless legs.

It was none of his business if a casual acquaintance cheated on his wife with some little... His jaw clenched, Seb turned away. Then she laughed again, the sound so light, so carefree, so damn sexy that something snapped inside him. First his mother, now this woman... Another selfish, beautiful woman who didn't give a damn about the collateral damage they caused as they went about pleasing themselves, leaving a trail of broken hearts and broken marriages in their destructive wake.

There was a corner of his mind where enough sanity lingered for him to know this was not a good idea, but it was a mere whisper compared to the din of the outrage hammering inside his skull as he strode across the grass, embracing the rage that was colder than the snowflakes that were falling in earnest now.

'So Alice couldn't make it tonight, Adrian...'

Mari struggled to keep her balance as Adrian let her go. No, had he *pushed* her away?

Adrian didn't see her hurt, questioning look; his attention was on the owner of the deep, harsh voice. Mari had to turn her head to bring the man into her line of vision.

Before she absorbed the details of the stranger's tall, impressively athletic frame, expensively tailored suit and face that was combined arrogance and beauty, Mari felt the raw power he exuded.

She felt it like a dark prickle under her skin as he turned his obsidian stare on her.

The tightness in her chest loosened when she managed to break contact with those incredibly penetrating pitch-black eyes—eyes that belonged to the most incredibly beautiful man she had ever seen.

Beside him, dark, brooding Adrian, whom she had fallen for as he read poetry in his beautiful voice looked less of both, almost...*soft*... She pushed away the disloyal thought and waited for Adrian to introduce her. Would he say *girlfriend*? It would be the first time; at college they had to be discreet. Students and lecturers dating was frowned on, though, as Adrian said, it happened all the time.

For some reason the fact she was even more beautiful up close increased the level of Seb's anger by several icy notches. Her eyes, kitten wide, were the deepest shade of violet blue he had ever seen, her mouth was lush and full and her satiny skin was almost translucent…and it turned out husband stealers could have freckles. The detail softened the sultry siren look into a deeply deceptive wholesome innocence.

'Mr… Seb… Well, this is…is…is…'

He let the stuttering loser, for once at a loss for words, suffer for a moment before suggesting ironically, *'Nice?'*

'This isn't what it looks like.' The cheating husband took another step to distance himself from the girl who was standing there, quite beautiful, quite still; she could have passed for a statue.

The music had stopped and everyone around them, sensing the drama, busily pretended not to be listening while hanging on every word. The girl moved towards her lover, who held out a hand as though to fend her off. She froze in response to the rejection, her big eyes radiating hurt and confusion. Seb thought of hard-working Alice, all the Alices out there, and cast out the seed of pity before it took root in his head.

'Is Alice… You know, your *wife*… Is she working, or is she looking after the kids? How does that woman cope?' He shook his head in wondering admiration and drawled, 'A busy medical practice, a mother of two and a husband who cheats on her?'

Mari waited for Adrian to say something, *willed* him to say something, to tell this terrible man who had appeared seemingly out of nowhere like some sort of sleek and dark avenging angel—in a world where angels wore very expensive tailoring—that this was all a mistake.

They'd laugh about it later in bed when they were sharing the bottle of champagne that he had ordered.

But the only sound was the shocked mutters from the other guests. Mari didn't turn her head, but she could feel the hostility and disapproval of their stares like daggers in her slender back.

'I couldn't help myself. *She*… I love my wife but… Well, just *look* at her!'

Her last hope vanished.

Every word that man had said was true.

She was the other woman. She hadn't known, but that didn't lessen Mari's sense of crushing guilt and shame. Her sense of total isolation was complete; she had never felt more alone in her life. Pressing a hand to her stomach, she breathed her way through a wave of intense nausea. When was Adrian going to tell her? *After, stupid.*

Seb, tuning out the rest of the other man's words, followed the line of his accusing finger. The woman standing there represented everything he despised in a female, yet he had no control over the hot hunger that slammed afresh through his body.

While his mind rejected and despised her, his body wanted her. You had to recognise a weakness to control it, and Seb valued control.

Control or not, it was still salt in a raw wound to acknowledge that she stood there looking like a piece of porcelain about to shatter, and there was a part of him that wanted to comfort her.

She could have had any man she wanted, and she had decided she wanted a married loser? When she could have... *Who, Seb? You?*

He ignored the mocking words in his head and launched a fresh invective, this time directed at the woman. 'Do you *care* that he's got a wife and children waiting for him at home?'

Mari cringed under the man's interrogative stare, literally paralysed by misery and guilt.

Her silence whipped his anger to a fresh high as he turned his inner rage on her and snarled contemptuously, 'Is it just a bit of fun?' He shook his dark head, a harsh sound of disgust escaping his clamped lips as he suggested with withering distaste, 'Or just because you can?'

She swayed and Seb heard the catch of her breath above the wind and the litany of excuses that were free falling from Adrian's lips, telling everyone who would listen how this was not his fault, he was a victim.

With an exasperated growl Seb turned his head and dealt the cheating husband an arctic glare. The other man gulped and whined.

'You won't tell Alice, will you? It'll only hurt her, and this will never happen again.'

'Wow, you really are a prize, aren't you?' Seb's attentions swivelled back to the girl. 'Did you think he would marry you, or is this real *love*?' he mocked. 'So that makes it all right?'

'I'm sorry.'

The whisper made Seb's tenuous grip on his self-control slip another fatal notch.

'Sorry...?' he blasted back, six feet five of towering contempt moving in a step closer. 'You think that makes it somehow better, that it makes the people whose lives you trashed happy again? Love or not, sweetheart, what you've done makes you the worst sort of slut... Oh, and just for the record, men take sluts to their beds, but rarely in my experience marry them.'

Every word the man was saying was true; every word was making something shrivel and die inside her.

With a final horrified stare from the swimming blue eyes, she gave a choked sob and turned and ran, her fiery hair streaming out behind her.

'You big bully!' An elderly grey-haired woman

voiced what seemed to be, if the glares were any indication, the general consensus.

The hell of it was Seb, who kept seeing those blue eyes, half agreed with them.

CHAPTER ONE

MARI HADN'T EXPECTED it to be this easy, but so far no one questioned her presence in the cordoned-off street where she blended in pretty well with the other women negotiating the ancient cobbles in high heels, worried that any slip or inelegant stumble would be recorded for posterity by the photographers lined up along the other side of the barrier.

She had more things than falling off her heels to worry about!

Relax, Mari. A ghost of a smile touched her lips—she was, after all, only following doctor's orders. Admittedly it was doubtful if the well-meaning medic had had *this* in mind when he had noticed her shaking hand was unable to hold a teacup and banned her from the hospital for twenty-four hours.

'We'll let you know if there is any change. Go home,' he had encouraged. 'Have a meal, get some rest. You need a change of scene and something to take your mind off things. I know it's hard, but you're in this for the long haul and you'll be no good to your brother if you collapse from exhaustion, believe me. I've seen it happen.'

If she'd had the energy Mari might have laughed at the thought of *anything* taking her mind off her brother's situation. But common sense had made her recognise the grain of truth in his words, so she'd not protested when he'd called her a taxi, not that she'd had any intention of being away from Mark's bedside for longer than it took her to shower and get a change of clothes.

After the shower she had sat looking at a sandwich she had no appetite for with the television playing in the background to drown out her thoughts… *If only?* Her brain wouldn't switch off; it just kept going around in dizzying circles. She managed a bite, chewing and swallowing without tasting before her eyes began to close, her chin sank to her chest and she was on the point of drifting off when she was jolted awake by a name. Hate pushed away fatigue as, her expression set in lines of loathing, she reached for the volume on the TV control.

The news presenter on the scene was giving the viewers the life story of the bride and groom in what was being grandly called 'the wedding of the year'.

God, was that today…?

Mari sat there, her hate an aching solid presence on her chest, her thoughts buzzing as she tuned out the woman who droned on while images of the bride looking beautiful somewhere fashionable and the groom—even more beautiful—looking down his aristocratic nose at someone or something flashed across the screen.

She knew all she needed to about Seb Rey-Defoe and his bride-to-be, and as far as she was concerned they deserved one another! When she had seen the announcement of their forthcoming wedding she had laughed.

The bride, Elise Hall-Prentice, was an upper-crust beauty whose claim to fame beyond her wardrobe and her social connections was being the star of a reality show that had involved her pretending to have lost all her money—*would she lose her friends*?

As if anyone cared! The woman had all the sincerity of a fake tan, and the empathy of a reptile, without the charm!

And this was *their* day, while Mark was lying in a hospital bed, and, thanks to that hateful man, if she died tomorrow she'd be a virgin while they'd have the perfect day. Nothing would *dare* go wrong.

It was so unfair!

But then life was unfair, she reflected, reaching for the control as the picture on the screen cut to VIP guests in flowing Arab gowns getting out of helicopters. She dropped the control, her eyes flying wide open... What if something or *someone* spoilt their perfect day? Her laugh was a mixture of fear and exhilaration as she thought—and *why not*?

Why should everything go *his* way? Why should he walk through life immune to the stuff that everyone else had to deal with, cushioned by money and power? Both her and Mark's lives had been touched, and not in a good way, by that man, and he had probably forgotten they existed—maybe it was time to remind him?

Suddenly no longer tired at all but filled with a sense of purpose, she went to the wardrobe and pulled out *the* blue dress and held it against herself as she looked critically at her mirror image. That man had humiliated her in public. *Let's see*, she thought grimly, *how he enjoys it when he's the one on the receiving end.*

'I just have to ask.'

Mari started violently as the young woman touched her arm, stepping back onto the neatly trimmed grass verge as a cluster of well-dressed people, their laughter sounding like a flock of seagulls, went by.

Convinced that her guilt was written across her forehead in neon letters, she waited, breath held, for the axe to fall. *Which it will if you don't start believing in yourself,* she told herself sternly.

'You've got to tell me, *who* are you wearing?'

The comment poked a tiny hole in Mari's grim focus, allowing a ghost of a wry smile to touch her full lips.

Her reply was honest. Honesty was the best policy. She pushed away the stab of unease. There were exceptions to every rule and occasions when breaking them was the right thing to do.

'I'm not sure.'

Another smile almost escaped. The woman's wide-eyed reaction suggested she was seeing Mari walk into a wardrobe crammed with designer outfits. In reality, nothing could be farther from the truth. She possessed one other dress beside this bargain designer second with the label cut out.

The blue silk shift that had excited the other woman's admiration left her arms bare and ended just above the knee. She liked the simplicity of the flattering figure-skimming cut, and the bright cerulean shade echoed the colour of her eyes almost exactly. People who got past her hair often commented on the colour of her eyes, frequently asking if she wore coloured contact lenses to achieve the dramatic shade.

'If I had your hair I wouldn't wear a hat either.' Her eyes on Mari's tumbling auburn curls, the young woman touched a rueful hand to the frothy pink confection perched jauntily on her smooth blonde hair as she responded to an irritable, 'Come on, Sue!' from a tall, grumpy-looking young man, top hat in hand.

He saw Mari, looked far less grumpy and adjusted his tie. Mari, oblivious to the male admiration, attempted to slip away but the young woman moved to block her way.

'Do you mind—can I have a picture for my blog?'

Before she could respond the woman was snapping Mari on her phone.

'Who was that?'

'I think she's that model…or the actress in what was that film, the one with…?'

Under normal circumstances the overheard snatch of conversation as she hurried on would have made Mari laugh, but this situation was not normal, and she couldn't allow herself to be distracted.

What would they say if they could share the

joke: not only was she not a famous model or actress, she was not even a guest at this wedding!

She was crashing it!

A thing that a month, a week, even a day ago, she could not have imagined herself doing.

A lot of things could change in a week!

A week ago Mari was listening to her twin brother telling her how his life was ruined, ignorant then of the real life-wrecking disaster that would strike him within the next few hours. At that moment disaster meant being dumped by the woman he loved because her very important brother, with his blue blood and family estates, didn't think that he, Mark Jones, who didn't even know who his parents were, was good enough for a Defoe!

Mari offered her sympathy, while in reality she was dizzy with relief. It was all she could do not to punch the air in triumph. The sick feeling that had been in the pit of her stomach ever since she had realised who her twin's new girlfriend's brother was had gone.

That her happiness came from her brother's misery made her feel terribly guilty, but the truth was, since she had realised that there was a strong possibility that Mark's new relationship might bring her face-to-face with the man who after six years still featured in her night-mares, she had been living with a sense of im-pending doom.

Crazy, really—for years she'd fantasised about coming face-to-face with him and telling him all the things she wished she had at the time, instead of just standing there and taking every vile insult he'd thrown at her... She had actu-ally apologised!

No matter how many times she tweaked the cathartic speech she longed to deliver, deep down she had always known this was only a fantasy, and the knowledge infuriated her. She had spent her life not only standing up for her-self, but also fighting the battles of anyone less able to fight for themselves, but there was no escaping the shameful fact that when the op-portunity had arisen for her to defend herself, she'd bottled it!

And run away rather than face things!

She could still remember years ago, how cold the wind had felt as she had dashed across the lawn into the hotel away from all those eyes and the people judging her.

'He was on the news tonight. Did you see him?'

'Who?' she asked, her thoughts still on that terrible night six years ago.

'Sebastian Rey-Defoe.'

The name made her tense and the awed way her brother said it made her want to scream. She could admire achievements, even when money and power were not things she personally felt any desire for, but to inherit a position and money… What was to admire about that? Any more than you could admire someone for being beautiful and brooding, for inheriting genes that gave him sculpted features, spectacular eyes and sensually moulded lips.

'They were talking about the massive deal he has with some Gulf state. The royal family there are putting up half the capital and one of his companies is supplying the know-how to computerise their health service, sort of a tit-for-tat thing—it could bring over a thousand jobs back to the area where they plan to build—'

Mari gave a cynical snort and cut across him. 'And line his pockets with money, too.'

Mark's sigh was tinged with envy. 'If only I had some money.'

'What's money got to do with it, and what does it matter what he thinks if you want to be together?'

'I don't know why I expected you to understand. I mean, you've never been in love, have you? Oh, I forgot—you go for married men, don't you…?'

Essentially a nice person, this was Mark when

he was hurting. He hit out, wanting to share his misery, and he usually succeeded because he knew her weak spots.

He was the only one who did know this particular weak spot. Not the shameful details—those she would never share with anyone—just the basics. Well, knocking on his door at 4:00 a.m., having lost her key during the terrible journey back from Cumbria that had involved trains, buses and multiple changes, had required an explanation of sorts.

'Adrian, he's married!' had been all she'd got out before she had burst into tears and fell sobbing through the door.

It was the past and she had moved on, Mari reminded herself.

Moved on or not, the fact remained that she couldn't think of her eighteen-year-old self without cringing. How had she ever been that naive, that...*needy*? How could she not have seen past the smooth, slick charm and macho posturing of her personal tutor?

'If you're not ready, Mari, I understand you want the first time to be special. I can wait...'

She had almost fallen over herself to assure Adrian that she *was* ready and she *loved* the Lake District. She'd never even had a boyfriend and here was this gorgeous, sophisticated man who looked like one of the Byronic heroes he lectured on falling for her, Mari Jones. Of course she couldn't wait to show him how much she loved him.

And she would have.

If *that* man hadn't appeared when he had…

For a year after the event he had been *that* man in her head, the strong, amazingly handsome lines of his lean face clearer somehow than Adrian's, until the day she had opened a magazine in the dentist's waiting room and there he was on a silver-sanded beach, too beautiful to be real, just like the blonde model he was entangled with.

The man who had humiliated her in front of an audience who had eaten up every word, every insult he had so eloquently delivered, was Sebastian Rey-Defoe: rich, gifted and born with several silver spoons in his cruel, insult-spewing mouth.

He'd made her feel grubby and guilty, his contempt somehow worse than Adrian's deceit; at least she'd got the chance to tell Adrian that he was a total sleaze.

That man had not paused to ask questions, he'd just presumed the very worst. It hadn't even crossed his mind that she might be a victim. Or she *would* have been—he'd saved her from her own ignorance and in the process made her a hell of a lot more cautious where men were concerned.

Done her a favour… Maybe…? That part had been accidental. He hadn't been saving her from anything; he had been there to judge, to serve her up on a platter for public condemnation.

The incident had left Mari unable to trust her own judgement, which had proved an obstacle when some *seemingly* nice guy had wanted to get serious… Yes, she had trust issues.

She'd taken the psych class and she knew a therapist would say her fear of rejection stemmed from being an abandoned baby, which was stupid because Mark shared her history and he tumbled in and out of love at the drop of a hat.

She glared at her brother now. 'You know, Mark, there are times when you can really be a vicious little—'

'Sorry, Mari.' Immediately contrite, her twin got up and came over, enfolding her in a hug. 'You know I didn't mean it. I don't know what I'm saying. Everything was going so great. I mean, I actually made money last month, though the loan was much appreciated, sis, and the weekend was perfect, it was another world, Mari, honestly you've no idea. She never said that her grandfather was a lord, and the house… They live on this incredible estate, Mandeville Hall. It turns out the Defoes came over with William the Conqueror or something and what are we?' His handsome face despondent now after the burst of envious enthusiasm, he sank back down into the chair.

'Lucky—we are lucky to have found a terrific foster family, people who cared about us.'

It had been third time lucky.

Initially there had been plenty of people eager to adopt the cute twin babies whose discovery on the doorstep of a church had captured the public imagination for about five minutes. There had still been plenty of interested would-be parents at the point some months later when the authorities had decided the babies' biological parents were not going to come forward to claim them.

Their enthusiasm had decreased when they had discovered that one of the babies, so pretty as a newborn, had developed a raft of allergies that gave the infant a constant cough and various unattractive rashes, kept under control only by a complicated prescription of numerous lotions and ointments.

If the twins had not come as a package deal, the rosy-cheeked blond-haired boy would have been easy to home, but the authority's policy was not to split twins. So the boy had been left behind with his problematic sister.

There had been two temporary foster homes before they had finally been taken in by the

Warings, a marvellous couple who had plastered a wall of their Victorian semi with photos of the dozens of happy children who had lived under their roof over the years, some for a short time, others like the twins growing up as part of the large extended family.

'Yeah, I know, count my blessings,' Mark drawled. 'Don't you ever get tired of counting them, Mari, being so damned *grateful* when our own mother left us on some step?'

'I'm sure she had her reasons.'

'I don't care why she did it.'

It was true, Mari knew it—he didn't care, and she envied her twin this attitude. He never asked himself why. Or, was it something about me...?

'The fact remains she did... Do you know that the Defoes can trace their lineage back to William the Conqueror?'

Mari gave a bored yawn. 'Yes, Mark, you mentioned it.'

Her twin missed the sarcasm. 'Now, *that's* the sort of background to be proud of.'

The envy in his voice made Mari's annoyance grow.

'I'm not ashamed of my background.' That was thanks to their foster parents; grateful didn't cover her attitude to the big-hearted couple.

'Neither am I,' Mark protested. 'But I was

thinking, Mari, perhaps if you could talk to the guy, make him see that we are not—'

The thought would have been laughable had it not been so horrific. 'No, I will not!'

'But—'

'Oh, for God's sake, Mark, grow a pair and stop wallowing!' The exasperated words were out before she could stop them.

Why hadn't she kept her mouth shut?

She pushed away the guilt. It wasn't *her* fault, it was *his*… Her eyes narrowed to midnight-blue slits. She felt light-headed with the depth of the hate she felt as she walked, confident and smiling, past the security guard and into the cathedral. She'd probably leave through the back door and definitely under escort from one of the numerous security guards, but it would be worth it.

The perfect wedding would have an ugly moment. The rest of their lives might be perfect, but there would be a tiny blemish, a moment when *he* would be the one being judged.

'You sure about this?'

The question from his best man made Seb lift his eyes from his contemplation of the stone floor.

'Just a joke.' Jake shifted uncomfortably under

the dark stare. 'Well, it's so final,' he tacked on defensively.

'Not always.'

It was hard to be objective but Seb thought his marriage stood a better chance than many, though his optimism was tinged with a healthy realism—you couldn't ignore divorce statistics—but he had avoided the usual traps that led to break-ups, the most obvious one being starting from the premise that love and passion were a basis for a successful marriage.

He did not have to look far to see the perfect proof of this. His parents had had and presumably still did have both, and their turbulent on-again, off-again union could not by any normal measure be called successful except by them, or the tabloids, whose circulation figures always leaped when the infamous pair married, divorced or decided to tell all.

The only thing the handsome polo player with little interest in the swathe of family acres in Argentina he had inherited had in common with the only child of a titled British aristocrat who knew how to party hard was a total lack of self-control and a selfish disregard for the consequences of their actions.

Not that the pair could be accused of not trying: they had been married three times, divorced twice and had both had several lovers in between. Seb had been born during their first marriage, and *rescued*, as he always thought of it, at age eight by his maternal grandfather during their short second marriage and brought to England to live. Had the loved-up pair noticed? Or had they been just a little bit relieved to have the child that demanded too much attention removed?

His half-sister, Fleur, the result of one of his mother's *in between* affairs, had been born at Mandeville and officially adopted by their grandfather. She barely had a relationship with the mother, who had left a week after the birth.

If in doubt Seb always asked himself what his parents would do, and did the opposite—and it had worked. When asked what he wanted to be when he grew up Seb had said *not my father*.

Seb's decision at eighteen to change his name by deed poll, adding his mother's maiden name to his Argentine father's, had been his attempt to say thank-you to the grandparent who had brought him up. Though there had been no display of emotion when he had told his grandfather, he knew without being told that the gesture had pleased him, as had his unspoken determination to reclaim the proud family name.

Seb had succeeded. When the Defoe family were spoken of now, 90 per cent of the time it was his own financial success that made the headlines, not the latest instalment in his parents' soap opera of a life. His life was not about to become a spin-off series! His marriage would not be an emotional roller coaster.

He knew that in his efforts to make the name Defoe one to be proud of he had gained a reputation for ruthlessness. But personal insults aside, no one had ever connected his name with anything underhand or sleazy, which was what mattered to Seb.

When people called him proud he did not take it as an insult. He *was* proud—proud of not compromising his principles and of making it work, making the Defoe name synonymous with fair dealing. And the reward had come with the incredible deal that he was about to pull off. A chance like this only came along once in a lifetime and while he hadn't planned this marriage for that reason, its timing had been perfect and probably, he suspected, swung the deal. The royal family were big on family values and believed a married man was more stable and dependable.

The idea that marriage could fundamentally change a man tugged the corners of his expressive lips upwards. Seb had no expectation or intention that marriage would change him; he saw no reason it should.

Success in marriage was about having realistic expectations; of course, there would be some compromises, and he had thought about them, but he was ready to make the commitment. He prided himself on his control and didn't for a second doubt his ability to be faithful.

His idea of marriage hell was what his parents had.

He just wished his grandfather were around to see today, that he could know that the Defoe name would live on, that he had kept his promise. It had been an easy promise to give, because Seb recognised the attraction of continuity, the opportunity of passing on the values his grandfather had given him.

He and Elise were on the same page. She agreed that stability and discipline were important for a child; they shared the same values, which was essential—in fact they rarely disagreed on any subject. She had even agreed to give up her career to bring up a family. Seb hadn't realised she had one, but he had been touched by the gesture.

Jake began to pace restlessly. 'God, I hate waiting… What if…? No, she'll turn up. You couldn't be that lucky… Sorry, I didn't mean… It's just…'

There was a short silence before the screen of dark lashes lifted from olive skin stretched tight

across the angle of Seb's slanted cheekbones.
His was a face with no softness in any aspect.

'Just what?'

'It's such a big step being responsible for
someone else, being with them every day.'

'Elise is not...clingy.' This understatement
caused Seb's mobile mouth to tug upwards at the
corners. 'We will both continue on with our lives
much as normal.' With no emotional dramas, no
raised voices or tabloid speculation.

'So why bother getting married?' Jake immediately looked embarrassed, adding to it by allowing his doubt to slip through into his voice
as he continued, 'Sorry, but you are happy...?'

Happy? Seb did not consider himself a natu-
rally happy person, and the constant pursuit of it
seemed to him exhausting. He lived in the present. 'I'll be happy when today is over.'

After the warmth of the sun outside, the inside
of the cavernous building was cool, lit by hun-
dreds of flickering candles and filled with the
almost overpowering scent of jasmine and lilies.

When she paused midway up the aisle the tension that had been building in her chest reached
the point where she was fighting for breath. Mari
felt as though she were drowning, standing in

the middle of this beautiful building filled with beautiful people.

They were here to witness a celebration; she was here to... *Oh, God, what am I doing?* Mari stood there, the adrenaline in her bloodstream screaming flight or fight. She could do neither: her feet were glued to the floor; her limbs felt weirdly disconnected from her body.

'Room for a small one here!'

The cheery cry dragged Mari back from the brink of a panic attack. Breathing deeply, she turned her head to see a woman in a very large hat was waving her hand.

'Thanks,' she murmured as the lady obligingly slid along the pew. She had just settled in her seat when the two men seated in the front pew rose.

'My son, Jake,' the woman said with maternal pride. 'You wouldn't know it to look at him, but he is a millionaire...a computer genius. He and Sebastian have been friends since they were at school.'

Mari wasn't looking at the lanky man with the shock of blond hair who looked embarrassed as he waved to his mother. Her attention was riveted on the figure beside him, her narrowed eyes channelling all her pent-up hate at those imposing broad shoulders, the strong neck and the dark head. He stood with his back to the guests, frustrating Mari's desire to see his face.

When the congregation rose, Mari, hating every hair on the back of his neck, reacted a few seconds later. Her legs were trembling; her throat was dry; she felt like someone standing on the edge of a cliff not sure if she was going to take that leap.

Her chin came up. She'd run once and regretted her cowardice. She wasn't going to run again!

A few moments later the bride glided by in a rustle of lace, satin and the merest suggestion of complacence in her smile—not that Mari saw, as she was the only person who didn't dutifully turn to admire the vision.

'Gct on with it, get on with it…' she muttered between clenched teeth.

The big-hat lady moved in closer. 'Are you all right, dear?' she asked, using the big hat as a fan.

Mari managed a ghost of a smile. 'Fine.' The service began and she breathed a soft, 'Finally!'

When she heard his voice for the first time, the cool, confident sound sent a shock wave of anger through her shaking body and burned away her last doubts as the memories came flooding back.

'For better, for worse,' she muttered, thinking, *Pardon the pun*!

When she tried later to recall the sequence of events that preceded her standing in the aisle, she couldn't. She had not a clue of how she got there but she did have a very clear memory of opening her mouth twice and nothing coming out.

The third time it did!

'Yes, I do, I object!'

CHAPTER TWO

MARI FELT ALMOST as shocked as the two-hundred-plus pairs of eyes that swivelled her way; the place had great acoustics.

'A lot, I object.' Aware her voice was fading away weakly, she squared her shoulders and bellowed in a voice that bounced off the walls like a sonic boom. *'A lot!'*

Poor grammar, but it was definitely an attention getter! She had the stage until presumably she was rugby tackled by the security guards, or sectioned under the Mental Health Act. What did it say—a danger to yourself or others? There was only one other she wanted to be a danger to, one other who... *Stop thinking, Mari. You've got your moment—don't let it slip away.*

'He...!' Her second dramatic pause was not intended. The last person in the place, the *only* one who hadn't yet turned did, and as her eyes impacted with the sloe-dark stare of her intended victim her throat dried to dust.

One word slipped through her head—*dangerous*!

In many ways he looked exactly as she remembered: proud, arrogant, actually with that thin-bridged nose, slashing sybaritic cheekbones and sensually moulded, cruel-looking mouth he looked positively pagan! What she *hadn't* remembered about six years ago, before he had turned on her like the jungle predator he reminded her of, was her own humiliating reaction to the blatant sexuality he exuded. Even her scalp had tingled with a sexual awareness that made the muscles low in her belly tighten—that hadn't changed either!

Shamed acknowledgement grabbed her, and for a vital moment Mari lost her focus; she *almost* forgot what she'd come here for. She lifted her chin and ignored the squirming liquid sensation in her stomach. She had come here to give him a taste of his own medicine, see how *he* liked being humiliated.

He didn't seem to appreciate the clever role reversal. The last thing he looked was humiliated. The heavy-lidded eyes that held hers were the eyes of an eagle looking at its prey.

She was no victim!

Not this time, and if he had any doubts… Mari dropped her chin, closed her eyes and exhaled a long shaky breath to compose herself.

Then, heart pumping, she lifted her head and stretched out a hand towards him, letting her fingers flutter.

'You can't do this, Sebastian,' she appealed, pressing the hand now to her stomach. 'Our baby, he will need a father.' As she said this she couldn't help but think of her own father. Where was he now?

The woman had had her audience in her pocket from the first throbbing syllable of heartbreak and desperation, and now Seb felt their attention switch to him, not giving him sufficient time to recover from the shock of recognition that had felt like the vibration of a shotgun blast when he'd turned and seen her standing there. While the aftershocks still reverberated in his skull, he schooled his expression into neutral—less damage control and more an unwillingness to provide entertainment for the masses.

He saw her lips move and read, *Do you know who I am?*

Know who she was…?

In other circumstances he might have laughed. The number of occasions when he had lost control in his adult life could be counted on the fingers of one hand, and he wasn't about to forget that particular one, or the woman responsible.

But even if by some miracle he could have

conveniently blanked the incident from his mind—it had not been one of his greatest moments—Seb could never have wiped the memory of that primal rush. It had electrified every cell of his body. He had never before or since experienced anything that came close to his response to her innate sensuality.

Did she bring out the same animal response in all men? Men who, unlike him, could not recognise the response as a weakness; men who allowed their passions to rule their lives.

Men who lacked his self-control—without it he might have been a man like his father.

No longer able to fight the compulsion, his eyes dropped, moving in a slow sweep that took in every aspect of her from the glorious flaming head of Pre-Raphaelite curls that framed her perfectly oval face to the length of her endless legs to the sleek, sinuous curves in between. Everything was accentuated by a dress that was probably illegal in several countries…or was that the body?

It was the lust that slammed through him—hard to imagine a less appropriate response in the circumstances—that brought reality like a boomerang rushing back to hit him squarely in the gut. He reacted to the weakness with an explosive rush of anger.

'What the hell do you think you're doing?'

As he flung out the question in the periphery of his vision he sensed movement coming from the row that was reserved for the royal party. Hell, this was a disaster. Where was Security and where had they been when she had strolled in?

Her smile, sheer, silky provocation, caused him to take an involuntary step forward, fury for a fatal split second blanking logic.

'Now *you* know what it feels like!' Mari flung with a bravado she was not feeling... Actually she was feeling really weird.

The last thing Mari saw before the dancing black dots joined up and for the first time in her life she fainted was those dark implacable eyes staring with skin-peeling intensity at her.

Before she hit the ground, Seb had been pretty sure that the graceful fainting stunt was just as phoney as the rest of her performance.

But she wasn't moving... If she had knocked herself out, he thought grimly, it would deprive him of the pleasure of making her choke on her words, though not even a full retraction would fix the damage she had just caused.

He had spent years making the Defoe name stand for something, a brand that inspired confidence, and now in a matter of seconds this woman had destroyed it.

Ironic really that he had thought his parents' absence—they had not been willing to inter-

rupt their world cruise for their son's wedding—
would guarantee a drama-free day.

Seconds ticked and the entire place collec-
tively held its breath, until Seb lost his fight
against the instinct to react—someone had to
do something!

Did it have *to be you*? asked the voice in his
head.

It was just as well that his grandfather was
not here.

One arm under her legs, the other around her
back, he heaved her into his arms, wondering
how many phones were capturing the moment.
The action seemed to break the group paralysis
in the place, and as people started shifting in
their seats it was filled with a low buzz of conversation that drowned out the soft groan of the
woman in his arms.

As her head fitted itself into the angle of his
shoulder her crazy cloud of fiery red hair went
just about everywhere. He spat a tendril out of
his mouth and, eyes flat with suppressed fury,
turned his head to look at her face, marvelling
than anything that looked so beautiful could
cause so much damage.

Her blue-veined eyelids fluttered but stayed
sealed, and with another little groan she said a
name that sounded like Mark.

Another victim...?

Amazingly, unconscious she looked *almost* vulnerable, a million miles from the vindictive drama queen of moments before.

Why the hell had she done it?

'Now *you* know what it feels like' suggested simple payback. Seb understood the attraction of revenge, but who waited *six* years? The possibilities ran through his head as he strode, the cynosure of all eyes, up the aisle towards his bride, the white-hot burning anger he struggled to contain battering at the insides of his skull, his arms full of crazy, delusional or plain evil but definitely sweet-smelling redheaded witch.

'Keep still!' he growled under his breath as she squirmed up against him, turning her body so that her breasts flattened against his chest.

When he came level with Elise his iron expression softened. He felt a stab of guilt that he hadn't given her a second thought, which made him a selfish bastard.

Poor Elise—if this was hard for him he could only imagine how she was feeling under her veil. If there was ever a moment when he would have excused a tantrum this was it, but she was conducting herself with a dignity that contrasted starkly with that of the woman who had just smashed the reputation he had spent years rebuilding. A sound of mingled disbelief and self-disgust vibrated in his throat because half his mind was occupied imagining her naked.

'Sorry.' His soft apology coincided with an audible lull in the buzz of conversation. There *might* have been someone in the most distant corner who hadn't heard the word, which would undoubtedly be construed as an admission of guilt, but he doubted it.

His jaw clenched. *Perfect!* Feeling frustration closing in on him, he glanced down at the cause and found a pair of glazed blue eyes looking up at him.

'I'm not sorry,' she whispered before the dark lashes framing them came down in a fluttering curtain against her smooth, very pale cheek. Then with a soft murmur, she burrowed in closer.

You will be, Seb thought, struggling to focus on anger rather than his indiscriminate hormones, which were acting independent of his brain to the squirmy, sensationally packaged softness in his arms.

Even without looking he could feel Elise's dagger stare behind her veil, and who could blame her? Certainly not him. He wasn't always as appreciative as he ought to be of her composure. He sent up a silent apology for ever having wished she'd show just a little more spontaneity, just occasionally. Ninety-nine out of a hundred women in her place would be having hysterics right now.

'Door, Jake…?'

His best man, who had been standing there, blinked as though emerging from a trance and grabbed the door to his right to allow Seb to pass through.

'Look after Elise,' Seb said as he went through. 'Take her…someplace, tell her I won't be long, oh, and send for—'

'Ahead of you there. We have three medics here. Anything else?'

'Any of them a psychiatrist?' Seb muttered, and responded to the handclasp on his shoulder with a nod. 'Is there somewhere, Father, that I can…?'

'This way.'

Seb followed the priest into a small anteroom. By the time he had laid the unconscious redhead on the small couch there, Jake arrived with a guest in tow who he introduced as—

'Tom, Lucy's fiancé—he's a trauma surgeon.'

Seb, who had little interest in the man's credentials, took his eyes off the girl long enough to shake the man's hand. 'Do you mind taking a look?' He turned to his best man. 'Jake, where is Elise?'

'How far along is the pregnancy?'

Seb's attention swung back to the other man,

his jaw clenched as he fought for control. *Get used to it, Seb, this won't be the first time.* If he lost control this woman would win...*as if she hadn't already*?

'I really wouldn't know. This woman is—' about to say she was a complete and total stranger, he stopped and finished sharply '—delusional.'

Not hanging around to see if he was believed, he turned to Jake, who responded to his inter-rogative look with, 'First left down the stairs, third door on the r...no, left.'

It was actually the right.

The room he entered was larger and less sparsely furnished than the one he had just left.

His bride, her veil thrown back, was standing looking lovely in front of a stained-glass win-dow. Her mother, a woman he had never warmed to, sat in a chair. She stopped speaking when he walked in, but the word *lawyer* hung in the air.

'Sandra...' He tipped his head in acknowl-edgement.

'I have never been so humiliated in my life!' she responded in a voice that never failed to jar on him.

Tell me about it, he thought, turning to his bride-to-be.

He watched her struggle to produce a brittle smile.

'You're a star,' he said warmly. 'First thing, none of what she said was true.'

The older woman snorted.

'Mother, that is not being helpful.' Elise held up a hand, a pained expression flickering across her face before the smile was back in place. 'Please, Seb, there is really no need for explanations. I thought you realised that. I have total faith in your ability to make this... *unpleasantness* go away.'

'Everyone has their price.'

His glance flickered towards the older woman. 'Thank you for that contribution, Sandra.' His sarcasm sailed right over the woman's head. 'I have done nothing to pay for.'

'Mother, Sebastian is more than capable of dealing with this.'

'He allowed it to happen.'

Seb ignored the shrill accusation from the older woman.

'Do you believe me, Elise?'

Her eyes slid from his. 'I think it's totally irrelevant whether this woman's accusations are true or false, Sebastian.'

'You are taking the possibility I got another woman pregnant and deserted her remarkably well,' he drawled.

'Would you prefer I acted the hurt victim?'

A small confident smile curved her lips as she asked the question.

He looked at the hand she had laid on his arm, and after a moment she removed it. The flush on her cheeks penetrating her perfect make-up, she gave a tight smile.

'Look, I know you share my dislike of… messy emotional scenes, but the way you're acting anyone would think you *wanted* me to make a scene.'

Good question. Well, do you, Seb?

'I could but where would that get either of us? I'm a realist—we both are. We need to get back in there, put a brave face on it and show the world that we're a team.'

As locker-room motivational speeches went, it wasn't bad.

'This is about damage limitation, but these things happen. Mother's right, just keep her quiet.'

Feeling like someone who was seeing something that had been there all along, he shook his head as though the action would clear his vision. It didn't.

'How do you expect me to do that?'

The serene mask slipped and she yelled, 'Oh, for God's sake, don't be so dense! Throw some bloody money at her—you've got enough! This is my day, and I refuse…' She took a deep breath and lowered her voice to a soft steely murmur as she clarified it. 'I totally refuse to let anything or anyone ruin it, especially some little tramp you got pregnant!'

'So let me get this straight—you will ignore my indiscretions and you expect I will return the favour?'

She blinked, her eyes widening in an attitude of exasperated surprise as she chided impatiently, 'Well, obviously, Sebastian. I didn't think that needed spelling out.'

His reflective smile was filled with self-mockery. 'I think perhaps I did.' He turned to the older woman. 'Do you mind leaving us?'

'I'm not—'

'Get out.' In a business setting the soft menace in his voice would not have surprised anyone—he was preceded by his reputation—but the women he addressed reacted with open-mouthed shock.

He waited for her to leave the room before he turned to his fiancée, searching her face. 'You're not in love with me?'

'Are you saying that I don't satisfy you in bed?'

'I'm not referring to your competence in the bedroom. I'm talking about...' He paused. It was a subject he was even less qualified than Elise to discuss. 'It was not a criticism, just a fact, and

I'm not in love with you either—that was never a problem—but it turns out I want more than you can give me.' He did not want slavish devotion or mad, undying passion, but at the bare minimum he wanted a wife who gave a damn if she thought he was fooling around.

'Something more… A threesome? Or…I'm very broad-minded, Sebastian.'

And I'm very rich, he thought, his lips curling into a grimace of self-disgust. 'Just what would I have to do, Elise, to make you find me unacceptable as a husband?'

'Why are you acting as though I'm the one who's done something wrong?'

'You're right,' he admitted heavily. He had been guilty of twisting the facts to fit. On the surface Elise had seemed to be the perfect wife and mother, and he hadn't looked any deeper than the surface. 'This is my fault. I really don't think I'm the marrying kind.'

An ugly look of astonished fury contorted Elise's face as she saw her gold-lined future vanishing. 'Are you jilting me?'

'Yes, I suppose I am.'

Seb had made any number of bad calls in his life but he might, he realised as he closed the door behind him a few painful minutes later, just have been saved making the worst one yet.

In theory a wife who didn't give a damn what you did so long as you kept her in big houses, designer handbags and diamonds was a certain type of man's perfect wife, and he had thought he was that man.

It turned out he wasn't.

Logic told him he had no real right to feel distaste at having her priorities spelled out so starkly. He could accept many things in a marriage or the lack of them, but it turned out mutual respect was not one of them.

CHAPTER THREE

'SEB!' HER HEELS loud on the ancient stone of the narrow corridor, Fleur Defoe hurried to catch up with the tall figure of her brother.

As she got level with him he turned his head to growl an impatient, 'Not now, Fleur.'

His sister caught his arm, breathless and brimming with curiosity and concern. 'What's going on?'

A faint ironic smile touched his lips, lightening the grimness of his taut hard-boned expression as he reluctantly paused and eased his shoulders against the lime-washed wall.

'I wish I knew.'

Had she read about the wedding and thought why not…or had something happened, a trigger of some sort? He did not discount the possibility she was acting for a third party. It wasn't as if he had any shortage of enemies… More than one would not be unhappy if his royal connection was severed.

'People are asking questions, Seb.'

His dark brows lifted as he sketched a quick cynical smile. 'And providing more than a few answers.'

'They're asking if there's going to be a wedding.'

He levered himself away from the wall and speculated out loud. 'Or she might simply be insane.'

'What?' asked Fleur, who was trotting to keep up with him as he strode out, dragging the tie from around his neck as he did so.

'No, there isn't going to be a wedding.'

'Are you all right?' Fleur couldn't decide whether she was relieved or disturbed that her handsome brother looked more abstracted than heartbroken.

'Fine.' Was it coincidental that the Far East deal was at a delicate stage in the negotiations? The royal family were relatively broad-minded and progressive but by their nature nervous of scandal…and half a dozen members of that family had been sitting out there watching that debacle.

He struggled not to replay the scene, knowing that anger was an indulgence he could not afford. He needed a clear head if he was going to at least salvage the deal of a lifetime, and for that he needed the facts, needed to know there

were no fresh little surprises waiting… Afterwards he could throttle the redhead, or maybe
kiss her, he mused, thinking of that mouth and
feeling a strong slug of lust.

An image of her face drifted into his head. It
had surprised him over the years how well he
remembered it, how deep an impression it had
made, though not as it turned out as deep as the
one he had apparently made on her…

'How did you meet?'

'Meet who?' he said, only half listening to
his sister, who was trying to keep up with him.

'Mari, Mark's sister.'

In the act of dragging a hand across his hair
he stopped midgesture and swung back. His sister, two steps behind, dug in her heels to avoid
a collision and looked up expectantly at him.

The furrow between his dark, strongly delineated brows deepened. 'Last month's boyfriend
Mark…?'

His forehead pleated in concentration as he
brought to mind the features of the young man
in question. Fleur's boyfriends were pretty in-
terchangeable. This one had been particularly
painfully eager to please and say the right thing.
Trading on a boyish smile that probably had an
appreciative audience, he'd made a pretty inept
attempt to sell his latest business venture.

'You make it sound like I— All right, yes,'

she admitted with a rueful grimace. 'He didn't last long. He started getting way too serious so I cooled things. She, Mari, is his twin, which is kind of cool.'

'You have met?'

Fleur shook her head. 'No, but he has photos of them, and that hair is pretty unmistakable, but why,' she puzzled, 'are you asking me? You must know that if you're…'

Seb clenched his jaw and bellowed, 'I'm not sleeping with her!'

'*Seriously?*' She encountered her brother's stony look and held up her hands in an attitude of defeat. 'Fine, I believe you.'

Which might, he reflected grimly, make her the only one.

'Why not?'

He slowed his step slightly and flung over his shoulder, 'Why not what?'

'Aren't you sleeping with her? She is kind of incredible looking.'

'Until a few minutes ago I was engaged and I have only met the mad woman once, six years ago.'

Fleur's eyes widened. '*Six…!* Wow, you must have made an impression! What did you do?'

Not nearly as much as he'd have liked to.

'She acted as though she hated you, Seb.'

'You noticed that, too, did you?'

'It didn't seem likely you were together. She's not really your type, is she?'

The disappointment in her voice struck a nerve. 'Sane, you mean,' he cut back, adding with a satiric bite, 'Are there any mental-health problems in your boyfriend's family?'

'He's not my boyfriend but actually he— *They* don't know. They were found on a church doorstep when they were babies. It was a big headline at the time—he had cuttings.'

'They don't know who their parents are?' He filed away the information; it might be useful but he doubted it.

Fleur shook her head. 'No, they've only got each other, a bit like us.'

The men's voices penetrated the fog that cushioned Mari's thoughts. It was confusing but comforting. She knew that any second it would clear; she also knew that she didn't want it to.

'So she's awake?'

Mari kept her eyes shut, but she could see the flicker of light through the delicate skin of her eyelids. She wished someone would open a window—the scent of chrysanthemums and incense hung uncomfortably heavily in the still air. The man who had spoken had a very deep voice. If it had a colour it would be rich, night-sky blue-black, and the tactile quality in it made the hairs on her nape tingle.

'Oh, yes, it was just a faint, no serious damage. She landed on someone's hat.'

'Thanks, I can deal from here.'

'You sure, Seb? I could stay…'

The rest of the interchange was too softly spoken for her to catch, but the sound of a door opening and closing sent a soft tickling rush of cooler air across her face.

'You might as well get up. I know you're faking it.'

The voice sounded bored. Mari felt her indignation stir lazily; she wasn't faking anything.

'What am I doing here?'

And where was here?

She slowly turned in the direction of the voice, realising her head was cushioned on a hard and dusty pillow thing. Teeth gritted, she prised her eyelids apart. They felt as though she had weights attached to her eyelashes. It took several blinks to bring the face of the man who spoke into focus. The only other person in the room, he was standing in front of a deep window, the sun shining through the stained glass behind him and surrounding his face with a halo of blue flickering light.

Even without the light show it was an incredible face. The combination of the starkly drawn

lines of a broad, high forehead, aristocratic
cheekbones and sensually sculpted mouth was
arresting, but it was the hard, brooding quality
in his stare that almost tipped her into panic.

'You took the words right out of my mouth,'
he drawled.

Then the panic made sense. It came rushing
back in full relentless detail without the protective cushion of adrenaline-heated anger.

She had done it. She really had! *Oh, God!*

Wasn't she meant to be feeling great or at least
vindicated? Seeing the villain on the receiving
end of the tit-for-tat payback wasn't as satisfy-
ing as she'd imagined.

Struggling to channel calm, she moistened
her lips with her tongue and cleared her throat.
'Shouldn't you be getting married?' The aura
of masculinity he projected was even more pronounced in the enclosed space of this room. It
had a skin-prickling quality that was very disturbing on more than one level.

'I *should* be, yes.'

She dragged her eyes off the small V of brown
skin where the top button of his shirt had come
adrift along with his tie, feeling pretty disgusted
with her indiscriminate hormones. 'You mean
you're not…?'

'It's called off—wasn't that the idea?' He
raised an eyebrow.

She brought her lashes down to shield herself from his hard interrogative stare. *Was it?* Beyond inflicting the humiliation he had not thought twice about subjecting her to, had she thought much at all…? She'd had a vague mental image of sweeping out, leaving him a crushed man…or at least one recognising that he had no right interfering in the lives of the Jones twins. Refusing to acknowledge the strong element of compulsion involved, she moved her resentful blue gaze up the long, lean, muscle-packed length of him.

Yeah, that really worked well!

It was hard to imagine anyone looking less crushed, and it wasn't just his tungsten physique. The man was cold steel through and through. Aware her glance was becoming a full-on stare slash drool, she took a deep breath and pulled herself into a sitting position. Both hands on her hair, she brushed the flaming strands back from her face and swung her legs over the edge of the couch.

'Not really.'

'So what exactly did you expect to happen?'

She shrugged and dodged his stare, thinking, *Good question, Mari.*

A muscle clenched in his lean cheek as he fought to retain a grip on his temper. 'So you hadn't thought that far ahead?'

'It never occurred to me that she'd let some-one as rich as you get away.' She heard his sharp intake of breath and looked up, projecting wary defiance. 'I'm not sorry.'

'So you said, but that could change.' His con-versational tone did not hide the warning. Mari hugged herself to ward off the sudden chill in the room.

He had not thought she could go any paler but she did. Her skin had a translucent qual-ity that was fascinating…or was that just him? He pushed away the thought—admitting there were any chinks in his control would have been admitting a weakness. Even in his teens, while his contemporaries were making fools of them-selves over girls, Seb had always prided himself on the fact women only pushed the buttons he wanted them to—he was no longer a teenager.

Her rounded chin with the suggestion of a cleft lifted another defiant notch as she met his stare head-on, her dramatic eyes glittering with defiance.

'Is that a threat?'

Seb watched one feathery brow arch. All her features had a clear-cut delicate quality except for her mouth, and that was just plain tempting.

'Oh, that was, by the way, a rhetorical ques-tion. I'm not stupid. If you're going to have me arrested just get on with it.'

Seb looked at the hands she held out towards him crossed at the wrists. 'Handcuffs aren't really my style,' he drawled. 'But maybe yours?'

What was his style?

The question and the image that drifted into her head brought with them a rush of scorching heat.

Where had *that* come from?

Feeling the shamed warmth flame in her cheeks, she wrenched her stare clear of his hands and his long elegant fingers that continued to exert an unhealthy fascination for her. Her lashes provided a protective screen of sorts as she rubbed her wrists while the illicit images kept popping into her head—in none of them was she fighting against the imprisonment of those strong fingers.

'You have a disgusting mind.' *It takes one, Mari, to know one.* 'I *knew* you'd be a bully!'

What hadn't been so obvious until this moment was that she was capable of such carnal thoughts. If they'd involved any other man but him Mari would have been quite relieved—it would have knocked on the head her growing conviction that, if not frigid, she had asexual leanings. As it was, a life of celibacy was infinitely preferable to being attracted to men like him… Were there any men like him?

'Being proved right seems to make you happy,

though some might call it a lucky break. You might have pulled your little stunt and then discovered I was actually a kind and warm-hearted person. Actually I feel quite flattered that I made such an impression on you six years ago.'

She laughed, a hard, scornful sound, and put her bare feet on the floor. 'I remember you the same way people remember a bad dose of food poisoning.' Her hair fell forward in a rippling wave that caught and held his fascinated gaze as she checked out under the couch, adding accusingly, 'Where are my shoes? I want to go home.'

'And it's that simple?'

Mari struggled to hide the flash of fear that sent a chill through her body. 'You can't stop me!' She caught her full lower lip between her teeth and looked up at him through her lashes, hating the quiver of uncertainty in her voice.

'I think you owe me some sort of explanation at least, don't you?'

'I owe you nothing!' she flared back.

'Do you seriously think you can pull a stunt like that and walk away? Think about it,' he suggested, walking across to the window, where a butterfly was helplessly battering its fragile wings against the glass. He opened it, nudging the insect towards freedom with his finger before he turned back to Mari, whose eyes had followed every move he made. 'Did someone put you up to this?'

The abrupt question made her blink. There was something hypnotic about the way he moved. 'I don't know what you're talking about. Oh, I get it, you're one of those people who see a conspiracy around every corner.' She flashed an understanding smile. 'I believe they call it paranoia.'

'You expect me to believe that after six...*six* years you decided to get your own back just because I spoilt your dirty weekend with your married lover?' He grimaced remembering Adrian, now the *ex*-husband of the local doctor. 'I can only hope that time and experience has improved your taste.'

She loosed a laugh, her chest swelling with indignation. *Experience*... One day she might meet a man who was willing to go at her pace, but that looked about as likely as winning the lottery at the moment.

'Just!' she yelled. 'It'll be your fault if I never...' Appalled by what she had almost blurted out, she closed her eyes. Maybe a better form of revenge would have been sticking him with some bills for the therapy she so obviously badly needed.

I'm so screwed up, she thought grimly, *that*

the only man I have even imagined myself in bed with in recent memory is him!

He arched a black brow. *'Never...?'*

She shook back her hair, struggling to force the words past the emotional lump in her throat. 'Nothing. You started this, you acted like judge, jury and executioner when you took it on yourself to humiliate me in front of—'

'Of a handful of people who didn't know you, not several hundred who do know me. If this *was* a tit for tat it was overkill. You may not have liked what I said, but it was the truth.'

'*Your* truth!' she flared, her eyes flashing. Nothing had changed—he was still the same judgemental creep.

'It's really hard to play the truth-and-justice card, angel face, when you just stood up in front of everyone back there and lied your beautiful head off.' His glance dropped to her flat stomach. 'Are you actually pregnant?'

'How dare you?'

'Dare...?' he echoed, loosing an incredulous laugh. 'You just stood up and told several hundred people that I'm the father of your unborn child...so yes, pardon me for being *crass*, but I do bloody dare!

'You do realise, I suppose, that a DNA test will prove definitively that I am not the father? If you suggest otherwise I have a team of very expensive lawyers who will sue you to hell and back and issue so many writs that no tabloid will print a word of the story, and I don't respond well to blackmail.'

'And I don't respond well to threats,' she countered contemptuously. 'And I'm *not* pregnant! And if I was,' she added on a horrified afterthought, 'you would be the *last* man in the world I would want as the father!'

The insult appeared to pass over his head. 'There is no baby?' One less complication to be dealt with.

She responded without thinking. 'I don't want children.'

His impressive shoulders moved in the slightest suggestion of a shrug. 'No maternal feelings?'

Mari knew very little about maternal feelings, but she did know there were a lot of children out there who needed homes, and few like her own foster parents who were willing to offer one. She had decided a long time ago that if she was ever in a position to offer a child a home, it would be one of those abandoned children.

'You can't help yourself, can you? You just love to judge.'

'It wasn't a judgement.' At least she was honest, he mused, his expression hardening as he thought of Elise's parting shot—*You think you know everything, but I had no intention of having a baby and ruining my figure!*

The combative silence stretched as blue eyes clashed with dark brown; it was approaching snapping point when there was a tap on the door.

Mari turned her head as the door swung inwards and the girl that Mark loved appeared. The photo on his phone had shown how pretty she was, but it hadn't captured her sheer vitality or the suggestion of mischief in her big brown eyes.

'Tea, two sugars, good for shock, and a sandwich, the best I could do.'

Seb resisted the temptation to mention he was the one who'd had the shock as he took the tray and balanced it on a deep slate windowsill.

'Hi.' She waved a hand in Mari's direction. 'How's Mark these days?'

The unexpected question felt like a raw wound being jabbed with a knife.

'About as well as you'd expect.' A sound half between a sob and a laugh escaped Mari's pale lips as she shivered from a chill that came from within before elaborating with a bitterness born of despair, 'For someone who's driven into a lamp post and been told he might never walk again.'

It was as though it happened in slow motion. The girl's pretty, vivid little face crumpled, but before the tears that filled her big brown eyes could fall she was in the shelter of her brother's protective arms and out of the room. Before he left he turned his head and the look he gave Mari was one that promised retribution and maybe, she thought, biting her own quivering lip, she might deserve it.

The heavy door was only partially closed. Mari could hear the sound of voices, but not what they were saying.

Tears threatened, lying in a heavy clogging lump in her throat as she looked around the room. The stark white walls were bare but for a couple of wall sconces holding half-burned candles. Other than the couch she sat on and a massive dark wood cupboard, the only other piece of furniture in the place was a spindle-backed chair.

She stiffened as the door opened then closed quietly. He did everything quietly, the closing of the door, the crossing the room with the sort of exaggerated care that someone who had had too much to drink uses, but it wasn't the effects of alcohol his slow, measured movements disguised, it was the anger he was holding in... *just*. Nobody under the influence could move like that, she decided, thinking jungle cat as she watched him.

He stopped just in front of her and waited. The

silence shredded her already frayed nerves, and Mari lasted about twenty seconds before she felt compelled to break it. The other option by that point was screaming.

'I didn't mean—' she blurted, then stopped. She hadn't come here to apologise again but it was true she hadn't meant to hurt the girl. The only thing Fleur Defoe was guilty of was having a manipulative brother. 'I didn't mean to upset your sister.' She bit the inside of her cheek and fought off a tide of guilt. 'Is she all right?'

Seb struggled to tamp down his anger with only moderate success. How the hell could she pretend to give a damn? 'Because you care so much? Look, have a go at me if you want to. I can take care of myself.' He leaned in closer, his voice dropping to a low menacing purr that decimated any nerve ending his physical proximity hadn't already sent into shock. 'But if you go after my sister, so help me, I'll go after you.'

'Am I meant to be scared?' If so it was working. Only pride kept her retreating from the dark, cold menace in his deep-set eyes. 'I didn't want to hurt your sister. I wanted to hurt *you*!'

Possibly too much honesty at this point, Mari, she thought as she waited nervously for his reaction. The fact he didn't react beyond elevating an eyebrow and looking thoughtful was baffling rather than comforting.

It was hard to retain dignity barefoot, especially in this dress, which had not been this tight across her hips the last time she'd worn it. It was the price you paid when your drug of choice was chocolate. Even in her heels she would have needed to tilt her head back to look him in the eyes; with nothing between the soles of her feet and the stone floor she felt… Well, Mari had once or twice wondered what it felt like to be petite and delicate. Now she had an idea, and she didn't like it.

Ignoring her stomach fluttering and her curling toes, she thought, *What's the worst he can do*? And wished she hadn't because her vivid imagination responded to the invite and kicked in big time!

Seb, his temper cooling, felt an unwelcome stab of admiration. Her regal attitude was totally at odds with her gloriously mussed hair and bare feet but, by God, she carried it off. His eyes of their own accord dropped, following the soft, undulating curves of her body that the blue silk dress she wore lovingly hugged. She had come to play the victim, but looking the way she did she had to have been typecast as sinful seductress.

'I didn't think she'd actually dump you.'

'Is that an apology?'

'No, it's…' She stopped, her eyes widening

fractionally as a possible explanation for the bride's reaction struck her. 'Have you done it before…but for real?'

His expression grew cold and contemptuous. 'It must be the company you keep, but a lot of people don't cheat.'

But do you? she wondered, watching as he responded to the imperative hum of a phone, which he slid from his pocket. He scanned the screen before punching something in and returning it to his pocket.

'I haven't got long.' He was not fooled by the polite request; underneath the diplomatic language it was a royal command—he was being asked to defend brand Defoe.

'Don't let me keep you.'

The pert reply caused his attention, which had drifted away, to focus back in on her. 'Was what you said about your brother true?'

She was outraged by the question. 'Why would I lie about that?'

'Why would you lie about me fathering your child?' he countered.

'I've told you.'

'I know, spoil my day, wasn't it?' He tipped his head and gave a slow handclap. 'Well, you succeeded in more ways than you can imagine.' He dropped his hands and subjected her to a scrutiny of skin-peeling intensity. 'What exactly happened to your brother?' Something that had triggered today's stunt?

'He…he…' Hearing the helpless wobble in her voice, she swallowed and blinked back the emotional tears that sprang to her eyes. 'Mark could end up in a wheelchair permanently.' A lot was still unknown, and Mari refused to think the worst. 'Why are you asking? You don't give a damn about him, do you?' she charged, glaring up at him with angry contempt.

'I wouldn't wish that on anyone,' he replied, wondering how he would react in the other man's position. He hoped to God he would never find out.

She gave a bitter laugh. 'Not even someone who doesn't have the right…right…bloodline to marry your sister?'

Seb's dark brows drew together in an astonished straight line above his masterful nose as he looked down at her. 'Back up…'

If only she could have, Mari thought wistfully, she would have responded quite literally to this request. A few more feet to distance herself from his overpowering physical presence would have been welcome but there was nowhere to go.

'Marry?'

Her teeth clenched at this display of unconvincing innocence. 'Don't bother with the act—I know what you did.'

Well, that makes one of us, he thought with a sardonic grimace. Every time she opened her mouth he felt as though he were being led deeper into a maze.

He released a long, slow, hissing breath, controlling his temper and the desire to grab her—and the hell of it was that, whatever his intentions, the moment he laid his hands on her it would change what hovered unacknowledged between them, taunting him, the way her mouth taunted him.

He had known it from the moment he saw her standing there in the church denouncing him to everyone who knew him. He wanted this woman, and if he touched her now that want would wipe out everything else.

Wasn't it supposed to be therapeutic to look into your heart? Not that his heart was the organ involved in this instance. Either way, he didn't feel better—he felt frustrated self-disgust.

'Work from the premise I don't have a clue what you're talking about.'

'They were in love.' She paused, distracted by the muscle that was clenching and unclenching in his lean cheek. 'Y…you,' she stuttered, thinking he should come with a shipping warning to stop females drifting into his magnetic field. 'You put an end to it because you're an arrogant snob who passes judgement on people he doesn't know. You have no heart!'

As the quivering accusation left her lips her scornful gaze slid to his chest. The image of her placing her hand on his warm skin, feeling his heart beat under her fingers, came from nowhere. Severely shaken, she shook her head to dislodge it and the warm feeling it induced.

His brows lifted. She was really rather glorious in full flow with that pouting mouth and those flashing eyes. 'If they were…in love, surely that wouldn't have been possible. Doesn't love conquer all?'

While he was innocent of the charge, Seb privately acknowledged that had there been any actual danger of Fleur marrying the rather insipid young man he had met he would have done his utmost to stop it, but he liked to think he would have been more subtle.

The thought of Fleur's reaction to an outright ban from him twitched the corners of his mouth upwards in the ghost of a wry smile.

Seeing it, Mari felt her temper fizz up all over again. 'This is just a joke to you, isn't it?' she accused, overflowing with a sense of righteous outrage. 'You don't even have the guts to admit what you did was because my brother doesn't have the right school tie and has worked for what he has rather than it being handed to him on a golden platter, and don't deny it,' she added breathlessly.

Nostrils flared, he gave a mirthless smile. 'I wasn't about to,' he promised grimly. The idea of him explaining himself to this red-haired virago with a chip on her shoulder the size of a forest offended him on more levels than he could count.

'Before she brought him home to meet you, everything was fine.'

'Relationships end every day.' He cut her off with an impatient gesture of his hand. 'You have decided that I am responsible for your brother's broken heart, I get that part of your delusion, but the rest? I'm a bit hazy where I fit in. He had an accident? What sort of accident?'

'Mark came to see me after he and Fleur split up. He was distraught when he left—if he hadn't been he'd never have been drinking.'

'He drank?'

Hearing the grim condemnation in his voice, she rushed to her twin's defence.

'He was only just over the limit.'

He greeted this weak defence with a thin smile of disdain.

'And there was fog…' Her voice trailed away; she knew there was no excuse. 'He never drinks and drives—normally—and he wouldn't have been doing so that night if you hadn't interfered. You're the reason it happened.'

And if you'd been more sympathetic? Mari closed her eyes and her ears to the voice of self-loathing in her head because she simply couldn't bear it.

He watched, fighting an unexpected flash of concern as she started to sway forward and back on her heels, her eyes closed. Concern he didn't want to feel roughened his voice as he asked abruptly, 'Are you all right?'

Her blue eyes opened. They glittered with un-shed tears and loathing. 'Don't worry, I'm not about to faint again.' She sniffed and wiped a hand across her damp eyes.

While Seb considered himself pretty immune to most female tears, the sniff made him feel... *Uneasy* was not the right word, but as he pushed away the suggestion that the prosaic action touched a tender spot he refused to acknowledge he settled for it.

'Sit down,' he urged, coating his concern in impatience, because actually giving a damn about a woman who had deliberately set out to cause chaos in his life would have been irrational, and he wasn't.

He just didn't want her to faint at his feet.

'I don't need to sit down,' she snapped back.

'I'm going home.' She took two steps before a voice said in her head, *Running away*?

Teeth clenched, she swung back. This time *she* would be the one to have the last word. 'Why should you carry on living your perfect life when because of you my brother's life is ruined?'

CHAPTER FOUR

'WE'LL LEAVE THE perfection of my life out of this conversation and while I don't doubt you need someone to blame for what has happened to your brother—'

Mari stiffened defensively and cut in, yelling angrily, '*You* are to blame.'

'What happened to your brother is tragic, but it is not the result of anything I did. *He* chose to drink, *he* chose to get behind the wheel of a car, *his* decision, *his* responsibility,' he intoned with steely implacability. 'It is pure luck that he didn't injure an innocent.'

Gnawing her lower lip, Mari lowered her gaze. He had said it; she had thought it. 'He loved your sister.'

'It was hardly the act of passion,' Seb derided contemptuously. 'It was the act of a weak man who didn't think of the consequences of his actions. It seems to be a family failing.'

'He's lying in a hospital bed!' she cried, wondering if the callous monster even had a heart.

'Which is sad, but he is the architect of his own downfall and I am just glad he has not taken my sister down with him.'

Mari wasn't even aware that her arm had lifted, moving in a swishing arc towards his face until, a few inches short of making contact with his lean cheek, fingers like iron curled around her wrist, forcing it away and back down to her side.

She didn't even give him the chance to release her hand; she started fighting, pulling frantically to wrench her hand free. When he did so she lifted her head very slowly, her wild hair falling back to reveal eyes that were wide and filled with hate, her skin flushed rosy, her lips parted as she panted for breath as though they'd just gone several rounds—everything was out of proportion with her and so, he realised, were the reactions she evoked in him.

He moved in a step, bringing their bodies closer. She didn't move, if anything she swayed towards him as though responding to some invisible cord that connected them. He watched, fascinated, as the blue of her eyes was almost swallowed up by the dramatic dilation of her pupils.

She had the most glorious mouth he had ever

seen, the sort of mouth that made a man want to taste. Quite suddenly, despite the deafening peal of warning bells in his ears, Seb couldn't think of a single reason why he shouldn't taste her.

One hand behind her head, he dragged her to him, then, tangling his fingers in the fiery mass of her hair, he hooked the thumb of his free hand under her chin. He dipped his head.

He felt her trembling as he moved his lips across her mouth before accepting the irresistible invitation of her soft, parted lips and plundering the soft, moist sweetness within.

The moment his mouth covered hers Mari's mind stopped functioning and the rest of her nervous system went into overdrive. Then she was kissing him back with combative hunger she had not known existed. Above the thundering of her heartbeat she heard a distant moan and didn't associate the raw, needy sound with her.

From somewhere, some small sane corner of her fevered brain, she found the strength to resist. She pushed hard against his chest and the kiss stopped almost as abruptly as it had begun. She staggered back, her breasts rising and falling in agitation.

'I hate you,' she shot out, wiping the back of her hand symbolically across her mouth.

He stood there looking down at her, managing

to look insultingly cool. Could he really turn it on and off like that…?

'So nothing has changed.'

Still shaking while he continued to act as though nothing much had just happened, she smoothed a hand over her hair, appalled, deeply ashamed and most of all bewildered at the wanton way she had responded. 'You kissed me!'

If she'd known that *that* was going to be the price of the last word Mari would have swallowed her pride and bolted when she had the chance!

'I'm not going to get a honeymoon. I think the least you owe me is a kiss,' he drawled while silently cursing his lack of control.

Cursing because she was the sort of woman with whom one taste was not enough, she was the sort of woman who, before a man knew it, he could not function with or without. She was the sort of woman he had spent his life avoiding.

'I wish I *had* hit you!' she fired back.

'The day is young.'

'And you're in a hurry,' she reminded him.

She watched as he turned his cuff and glanced down at the metal-banded watch wrapped around his wrist. 'I am,' he agreed. 'Just one question, I'm curious. Do you think it was worth it?'

'Worth what?'

'Worth what is going to happen next.' He shook his head and looked incredulously at her. 'You really haven't thought your little revenge plan through, have you?' When she continued to look blank he elevated a dark brow. 'You just told people we were an item and you're pregnant. It won't stop there. There will be consequences beyond a bad moment in my *sooo* perfect life.' She carried on looking confused so he spelled it out. 'For you.'

She lifted her chin but he could see the uncertainty she couldn't hide in her eyes.

'What consequences?' she scoffed uneasily.

He didn't reply immediately; instead he left a space for her anxiety to climb.

There was amused contempt in the eyes that brushed her face. 'How many phones do you think caught part or all of your little drama? You have your five minutes of fame.'

A look of horror slowly spread across her face. 'I don't want it.'

'Tough. It's not optional.'

Her pallor exaggerated the sprinkling of freckles across the bridge of her small straight nose.

He remembered those freckles.

'I almost feel sorry for you.'

'I don't need your pity,' she flared back, eyes flashing.

One dark brow lifted. 'I said *almost.* I save my sympathy for those who deserve it. You chose to have an affair with a married man.' He disposed of her historical gripe with a dismissive click of his long fingers. 'You chose to make a spectacle of yourself in public, your brother chose to drink and get behind the wheel of a car. Instead of bleating, perhaps you should both man up.'

Of their own volition his dark eyes dropped. Anything less manlike than her heaving breasts outlined beneath the blue fabric that moulded them lovingly would have been hard to imagine. He didn't waste his time analysing the lustful surge of his body; he was working too hard at ignoring it.

'I *chose,*' she said, emphasising the word, 'to make a spectacle of *you*, and in that I'd say I have been very successful.' Almost mastering her struggle to appear indifferent, she shrugged and took the slim phone from her pocket.

'What are you doing?'

'Ringing for a taxi.' Eyes hard, she sketched a saccharine-sweet smile. 'I think I've imposed enough on your hospitality.'

He strolled to the door, pausing with his hand on the handle. 'Your shoes are on the window-sill, and your hat.'

'I don't have a hat.'

His eyes went to her hair before, face set, he

removed his gaze from the fascinating flame-red curls. 'Of course you don't. That would mean you stand the tiny risk of not being the centre of attention when you walk into a room.'

The suggestion that she wanted attention was so unexpected she struggled to think of a suitable response.

'I'd book your taxi for the east gate if you *really* don't want that fame…but you're only delaying the inevitable, sweetheart.'

With that parting shot he left without a backward glance.

The hospital car park was full. Mari drove around three times before she finally found herself a space in an overflow area, or *almost* a space. The one she backed her old Beetle into was so narrow that to get out she had to breathe in to squeeze her way between the car and wall, managing to scrape her knees against the brick wall as she did so.

Without a lot of interest she viewed the damage, the nuisance value of her torn trousers barely registering against the oppressive weight of the real disasters she was dealing with—some of her own making. At times it felt as if she were drowning…but mostly she managed to tread water.

It was two days since the event that had triggered the media storm and by some miracle Mark hadn't discovered what she'd done. That was the plus in what had been a nightmare weekend. Sebastian, with his sinister predictions of *consequences*, had been proved horribly right.

Mari was paying big time for her moment of madness.

She had been horrified when she had got out of the taxi to find a local reporter and photographer waiting. Head bent, she had not responded to the battery of questions or appeals for a quote.

Ironic now that she had thought that was bad—an hour later the duo had been joined by a dozen more from the nationals.

She had closed her curtains, ignored the notes shoved under the doors and turned off her phone, but she hadn't been able to resist the masochistic impulse to go online. There she had discovered the predictable photos posted on numerous sites, and unlike most of the comments, which had been almost universally negative, some had been flattering, especially the one that had gone viral of Sebastian looking impossibly handsome and noble carrying her looking like some sort of ginger Sleeping Beauty up the aisle.

On a lighter note she had discovered an amusingly written piece, which included a detailed, itemised and hilariously inaccurate breakdown of how much her outfit had cost on the—it turned out—much-read fashion blog of the woman who Mari had almost forgotten had admired her outfit on the way into church.

This had spawned several much darker spin-offs that itemised not only how much her clothes had cost but how much she had cost! It seemed that according to 'experts' very few of her body parts were the ones she had been born with! She'd had a nose job, cheek and lip implants... opinion was split on her breasts!

It was universally agreed that Sebastian had footed the bill to turn her into his *perfect woman*.

The phrase had been picked up by a Sunday tabloid that recognised headline gold when they saw it. They had put the words above two shots of her, one in the supposedly ultraexpensive wedding outfit, the other taken Saturday morning when, bleary eyed in her pyjamas, her hair a wild mess and looking slightly demented, she had opened the door and faced a battery of flashes.

But she had taken control and stopped acting like a victim. The turning point had come about two o'clock that morning when she had found herself reaching for the tablet on her bedside table. What else was there to do when you couldn't sleep but to get up to date with the latest vile names people were calling you and what awful things they were saying about you? The tablet propped on her lap, she had stopped and asked herself, *What are you doing, Mari*?

She could not control what people wrote but that didn't mean she had to read it! The light at the end of the tunnel was that presumably there would come a time when people would get bored with talking about her breasts. Until then she was going to walk around with her head held high.

And that morning, when the number of press outside the building where she lived had decreased, it looked as if she had survived the worst, or so she'd thought.

But the hits kept coming!

She lifted her chin. As tempting as it was to just give up and admit defeat, it wasn't an option. Mark needed her support. She pushed a strand of hair that had escaped the loose plait that hung down her back and glanced down... All dressed up, or in this case down, and nowhere to go.

But that might work to her advantage, she reflected, viewing her typical workday outfit of narrow-legged tailored trousers, teamed with leather pumps and a classic white shirt that she had put on this morning when she'd thought today was going to be a normal workday.

Still the professional look might make the doctors inclined to be more forthcoming with information than when she was wearing a

T-shirt and jeans. Either way she needed more information than they had so far given her, and Mark, who had been deeply depressed last night, had responded to all her questions with a defeatist shrug. It hadn't helped that she'd been really late, having changed taxis three times to avoid being followed to the hospital by the press—at least hospital security protected him.

She fingered the knot of the red silk scarf she wore tied around her throat while she dabbed a tissue to the blood seeping through the superficial break in the skin.

Finding herself unexpectedly free, she had hoped to catch the doctors after their morning rounds, but with the congestion in town and the time it had taken her to park that looked less likely. Still, it was worth a try. Throwing her plait over her shoulder, she started to jog.

People stared, but Mari decided that she could cope with a few raised eyebrows after the past few days. She kept up the energetic pace until she was outside the ward, then, consciously smoothing the frown lines from her brow along with the self-pitying thoughts before struggling hard to channel cheerful and optimistic, she advanced, passing the empty nurses' station en route to the side room where her brother had been since he had been transferred from the high dependency unit.

Her mood improved fractionally when she saw a group of suited figures—the doctors were still in the ward. As she approached, trying to identify her brother's consultant the men appeared not to notice her, then one turned and she froze, doing what she later suspected had looked like a 'rabbit in the headlights' impression.

He tilted his head in an attitude of distant recognition and Mari's shaky-kneed trepidation evaporated in a flash of white-hot fury. In a heartbeat she reached the group bristling antagonism and hostility, her decision that if she ever met him again she would be cool and disinterested blasted away in the silent explosion of anger.

'What are *you* doing here?' Possibilities zipped through her mind. Had he assumed that Mark was behind her actions and he'd come to confront him?

The small group fell silent, aware of the undercurrents but politely pretending they weren't.

'Miss Jones, twice in three days. Aren't I the lucky one? How delightful.' He turned to the other men. 'Does everyone know Miss Jones?'

'I asked you a question.'

'I have been visiting your brother.'

Wildly Mari looked past him, just able to make out her brother propped up in bed through the obscured glass panels.

'You know the hospital administrator, Mr Parkinson, and head of—'

Mari, ignoring the other men, cut him off before he made any further introductions.

'If you think you can obviate your guilt by bringing him a bunch of grapes, think again.'

'I do not feel guilty.'

'And that makes you a prize p—' She bit back the insult, struggling to get a grip on her temper. Not easy when every time she looked at this man standing there so elegant, projecting an effortless aura of cool command, so infuriatingly complacent and so sure, so damned *up himself*…! 'I would be grateful if you'd keep the hell away from my brother.'

The words were coated with ice, but Seb could almost see the flames licking just below the surface. Previously he had always discounted the red-haired temper thing as an example of an urban myth.

'Isn't that his choice, not yours?' Was she equally passionate in bed…? A nerve beside his mouth clenched as he struggled to tear his eyes from the plump curve of her lips.

The sort of woman you avoid, Seb, remember.

Mari, who was stabbing a shaky, accusing finger towards his broad chest, didn't notice the darkening of his eyes. She was too busy coping with the tingling aftershocks following the initial electrical charge that had taken away her breath in that first moment of recognition. She looked anywhere, everywhere but his mouth.

On top of everything else she could not deal with that kiss; the fact he'd kissed her or, most disturbing, that she'd liked it!

'If you have upset him so help me…' *You'll what, Mari?* Frustration gnawed at her as an overwhelming tidal wave of helplessness washed over her. Control in every part of her life seemed to be slipping through her fingers like sand.

'He seemed in a pretty positive frame of mind when I left him.'

She willed herself not to react to the provocation she saw in his silky smile as he continued to meet her spitting hostility and suspicion with a pleasant civility that probably made her look totally demented to the watching group—maybe she was! It was hard to call her behaviour over the past few days balanced and rational.

He wouldn't have been human if he hadn't taken a certain amount of malicious satisfaction from the knowledge he wasn't the only one having his life turned into a circus. At least he had the means, the expertise and experience to cushion himself and his family to a great extent from press intrusion, a luxury Mari Jones did not have.

Seb knew how fickle and unpredictable public opinion could be, so it was no major surprise that, by and large, coverage had mostly been pretty negative towards Mari Jones, but the toxic level of vitriol aimed her way had surprised him. He by comparison had for once escaped relatively lightly, partly due to the fact that Elise, who had wasted little time selling her 'jilted bride' sob story to the highest bidder, had chosen to play the victim and given a very inventive account of the woman who had stolen him from her.

His critical narrowed glance stilled on the smudges under her eyes that stood out darkly against her pallor before he looked away, reminding himself that any sleepless night she had she had more than earned—in making him the monster she had made herself the victim.

'How about you, Mari? Are you having a good day?'

Mari lifted her chin. She could hear the malicious mockery in his voice, even if no one else could.

She gazed up at him, feeling a loathing that she had not known she was capable of. 'I told myself it couldn't get worse but here you are...'

Mari hadn't been spared his presence. Even on the rare occasions she had managed to drift off into a light troubled sleep he'd been there every night. She was grateful that the details of those feverish dreams had slipped away but the snatches that lingered left a heavy visceral sensation of discomfort in the pit of her stomach.

'Well, this has been delightful catching up, Miss Jones,' he said with false sincerity designed to aggravate and annoy. The regret he expressed as he glanced towards the suits who had tactfully moved out of hearing distance was equally false and teeth clenching. 'I'd love to stay and chat but I'm afraid…'

Mari watched, a hundred insults unsaid as he calmly strolled away without a backward glance, the message clear in the set of his broad shoulders: she was dismissed. She was unimportant; she didn't even register on his radar.

Do you want to?

Ignoring this unhelpful intrusion from her mind, she stood there fighting a self-destructive impulse to chase after him. As much as she really wanted the last word, she knew it would come at a price.

Even thinking about the price last time sent her pulse racing. She had precious little dignity left, so she didn't want to throw away what she had for the satisfaction of telling him what she thought of him.

Gathering her wits, she stood for a few moments after the group, with Seb's dark head clearly visible above the heads of the shorter men, had vanished through a swinging door.

Hiding her trepidation under a cheery smile, she stepped into her brother's room. 'Hello, how are you feeling?'

The previous day Mark's mood had see-sawed between apathy and anger, so it was an intense relief to see the animation in his face.

'So you look better.' If her voice sounded too bright Mark didn't notice.

'I am feeling quite good… Take a look at this, Mari.'

Mari took a seat and began to flick through the glossy brochure that he handed her.

'Do you see what it says about this place? Just look at the statistics, Mari.' Eagerly he watched her face. 'Impressive or what?'

Mari grunted. She was looking at the fees, and there were numbers there that made her heart sink like a stone. 'Where did this come from, Mark?' She could not imagine that the hospital went around touting customers for this very expensive private clinic.

'Oh, I had a visitor—he left it for me to look at. Fleur's brother.'

Mari managed an expression of surprise, which her brother responded to with a laugh.

'I know, coincidence or what? It turns out he's on the hospital board or something. He said that this place has 24/7, one-to-one intensive therapy, all the latest technology.'

She put down the booklet with a sigh. 'Oh, God, Mark, you know there's no way we can afford this.' And it was hard to think of what had motivated Sebastian Defoe to give Mark this unless it was malice.

Was he really that cruel or vengeful?

And why was she even putting a question mark after the thought? He obviously was!

A determined look that Mari recognised all too well slid into her twin's eyes. 'There has to be a way—*your* credit rating is good...'

Mari, the phone call from the head teacher still very much on her mind, hated bringing her twin back down to earth. 'You know my job doesn't pay that sort of money, Mark.' Nobody went into teaching for the salary. 'I barely make ends meet as it is.'

'We could sell something.'

Mari's heart broke for him. 'Look, Mark, I'll do what I can, but I doubt very much in the meantime—'

'I could ask Fleur. Her family is loaded, and Fleur was always saying her big brother takes the responsibility stuff seriously—giving back to the community and all that.'

'His sister said that?'

Mark, propped up on his pillows, shrugged.

'Yeah, well, it's all about appearances, isn't it? And he can afford it. I thought *you* could have a word, mention how upset I was after Fleur broke up with me... Don't blame her or anything, as I get the feeling he's kind of protective, but—'

'I really don't think that would be a good idea,' Mari, horrified by what she was hearing, interrupted.

'Don't look like that. I'm not asking you to ask him straight out for money—you can be more subtle than that. You know, play up the sob story, flutter your eyelashes, do the weak girlie thing.'

Mari got to her feet; she was feeling sick. 'I couldn't do that.'

'You'd prefer that I end up in a wheelchair for life!'

'That doesn't have to happen, Mark. You know that the doctors have said with hard work and determination... I know it's a long haul, but I'll be with you every step of the way.'

'Why does it always have to be hard work? I know you're proud to be poor and everything, but I'm not. Why shouldn't I have it easy for once in my life? I have never asked you for anything in my life, Mari...' He saw her expression and stopped. 'All right, maybe a couple of times.'

Mari picked up the brochure. 'I'll see if I can

work something out, but I'm not begging for money from Sebastian Defoe.'

'You're too proud to beg?'

'It's not about pride, Mark.'

'Yes, it is!' he flared back bitterly. 'You've always been the same. You can't ask for help. You always have to do things the hard way. Well, it's easy for you to have pride—you can walk out of here.'

Her brother held her eyes for ten silent reproachful seconds before he turned his face to the wall.

'Mark, I'm sorry.'

Almost in tears, Mari left five minutes later, Mark still refusing point-blank to speak to her. He hadn't given her the silent treatment since they were children, and then sometimes he had kept it up for days.

As she walked along the hospital corridors Mari struggled to think past the awful sense of helplessness. She couldn't get the image of the silent reproach in her brother's eyes out of her head and it left her with a sick sense of helplessness that was crushing.

The doctor had caught Mari before she left the ward. She had really struggled to respond positively when he'd pronounced himself cautiously optimistic about her brother's prognosis;

he'd gone on to emphasise how important a positive mental attitude was in these cases and how easy it was for patients to become depressed.

Outside she took several deep gulps of fresh air. Mark was right: she could go home but he couldn't.

As much as she loved her twin she was perfectly aware that his impatience meant he always went for the quick fix. Their foster parents used to tell him there was no magic pill that cut out the hard work, but now he was convinced there was a magic pill. A carrot had been dangled and he couldn't have it, but while he knew it was there he'd never settle for hard slog.

Lost in her own thoughts, she barely noticed the drizzle that had begun to fall as she cut across the bay reserved for ambulances, and then across a half-empty area with reserved parking spaces, people who were too important to make the long trek to the overflow parking area for the hospitals.

'So how was your brother?'

Mari let out a shriek as the tall figure vaulted from a low-slung car that had *power statement* written all over it.

Had he been waiting for her? It didn't matter—she had a chance to tell him what she thought of him.

'Are you some sort of sadist?'

The sight of her walking out of the building had shaken loose an emotion that he hadn't wanted to acknowledge. Her body language had been so defeated, her slender shoulders so hunched she had looked as though it was an effort to put one foot in front of the other.

The contrast now as she stared up at him, blue eyes blazing, bosom heaving, her sensational, soft, full lips quivering with emotion as she launched into attack mode, was dramatic.

Seb was a man who valued control and moderation but she really was made for full-blown passionate excess… She was stunning, but then so was a hurricane, and he had never felt the desire to chase one or throw himself blindly into its path. Encounters with hurricanes needed to be carefully planned.

'I like that in you—you waste no time on pleasantries. You get right to the point. I'm the same way myself,' he drawled. 'It saves so much time.' He held open the door of his car, revealing the plush leather-clad interior. 'Do you want to sit down and catch your breath?'

'You don't make me breathless!' Exasperated that her response had managed to imply the exact opposite, she gritted her teeth.

'Really?'

She stuck out her chin and stubbornly held his eyes. 'Yes, really.'

'I must be losing my touch.'

'Oh, I don't know about that. You seem to be on top form,' she sneered angrily. 'Presumably seeing my brother in a hospital bed wasn't good or rather *bad* enough for you? No, *you* have to raise his hopes and leave me to crush them,' she choked, fighting back a sudden sob and finishing on a shaky quiver of husky despair. 'I'm sick of being the bad guy.'

Catching the thoughtful expression in his watchful dark eyes, she immediately regretted the bitter addition, and you couldn't really compare this situation with all the little things like telling Mark he couldn't ask their foster parents for the expensive trainers he wanted when they were kids.

'Then why do you let him do it?'

Thrown off balance by the soft question, she stared at him. 'What are you talking about?'

'Why do you let your brother play you like…? Whichever way you look at it, it isn't healthy—a grown man letting his sister fight his battles.' He shook his head. 'It's emasculating, not to mention manipulative.'

The casually voiced observation whipped angry colour into her cheeks. 'Are you calling me manipulative?' she asked in a low, dangerous voice.

'No, I'm calling your brother manipulative.'

Immediately defensive, Mari lifted her chin. 'My brother didn't…doesn't know about me crashing your wedding.' She bit her lip and added with a husky question mark, 'I'd like it to stay that way?'

This was not news to Seb, who considered himself a pretty good judge and had recognised the shallow insincerity behind Mark's smile the moment they had met. If the brother had known he had no doubt the younger man would have immediately tried to distance himself from his sister's actions.

'So you're asking a favour from me…?'

She shrugged and said in a flat little voice, 'Stupid idea.'

Experiencing an inexplicable impulse to live down to her expectations of him, he almost asked, 'What's it worth?'

Instead he found himself extending his hand.

Not in the plan, Seb, said the voice in his head.

Mari drew a tense breath but didn't step back. She couldn't—her feet were nailed to the floor. She stood there quivering as he touched her cheek, only lightly with his forefinger, but there was an element of compulsion about the way he drew a line down the soft downy curve of her cheek, his eyes following the action—then he repeated it.

'You think I put a price on everything?'

Hot desire pulsed through her body. Her response to the casual intimacy was frightening, exciting and humiliating all at once. It was so tiring fighting, not just him but the way he made her feel. For a split second she let herself wonder what it would be like to stop fighting.

'Don't you?' she asked, her reaction as his hand fell away ambivalent at best.

'I won't tell your brother about your wedding-crashing exploits.'

'Thank you.' Her relief was heartfelt, but her worried frown lingered. He said that now, but what if he changed his mind?

'Don't worry, I'm considered a man of my word.' He saw her eyes widen in alarm and gave a low chuckle. 'You really should never ever play poker.' Unless it was not for money and with him, he thought, warming quite literally to the idea of a slow striptease.

'I know Mark is bound to find out sometime,' she admitted. 'But it would be easier later. He's not even speaking to me right now.'

'You know, if you're not careful you'll spend your life—' He shook his head and finished abruptly. 'No, correction, you won't have a life of your own.' The thought made him angry.

Confused by the strength of the disapproval she could feel coming off him in waves, she arched an interrogative brow. 'And you care why exactly?'

A startled look chased across his lean face. 'I don't,' he denied, and shrugged. 'For all I know you enjoy it. Maybe it's symbiotic.' Displaying his white teeth in a smile that didn't reach his deep-set eyes, he leaned in and flicked her cheek with his finger. This time there was nothing seductive about the gesture. 'Slice Mari Jones and you'll find martyr running all the way through.'

She turned her chin away, hating his sneering suggestion and the way her body was betraying her by reacting to the sensual aura he projected.

'Slice Sebastian Rey-Defoe and you'll find sadistic bastard all the way through?' she countered angrily. 'You knew when you gave Mark the details of that place that we don't have the sort of money that it costs—you expect me to believe you did that out of the goodness of your heart?'

Was his cruelty casual or calculated? Mari couldn't decide which was worse.

'I'll pay for the treatment.'

CHAPTER FIVE

HOPE FLARED BUT was immediately swallowed up by a depressing wave of realism. He was no fairy godmother. It would be hard to think of a less appropriate analogy, even if he had been oozing the milk of human kindness instead of a headache-inducing level of testosterone.

'And afterwards,' he continued, 'I will fund any physical therapy and aftercare.'

When things sounded too good to be true there was often a very good reason.

'Why?'

She was unable to stop herself—her hostile gaze slid up the impeccably tailored length of him, but she knew during the journey over dark grey suit, white shirt and narrow burgundy tie that it wasn't hostility that made her stomach muscles tighten and quiver, which was stupid because she had never gone for the 'groomed to within an inch of his life' look. It always suggested a vanity that she didn't find attractive.

And he was so groomed he could have stepped right out of one of those glossy ads, the sort that suggested that if you bought the car, the fragrance, the shampoo, you, too, could look like this.

Only you wouldn't. There might be a few pale imitations but Sebastian was definitely a one-off, and in her opinion one too many. All the same, to look at him was… She just stopped herself sighing; the light flush along the high, smooth curve of her cheekbones she could not control… He would have been easier to tolerate had there been a single thing to criticise. Physical perfection when it came with a massive sense of superiority was not attractive.

Tell that to your hormones, Mari.

The suggestion of a smile touched his expressive lips as he studied her face. 'Don't worry, there are no strings.'

She lifted a hand to brush away the heavy strand of dark red hair that a gust of wind had plastered across her face, the same gust that ruffled his close-cropped dark hair up into attractive spikes.

'I wouldn't accept charity from you if my life depended on it!' she told him in a clear, confident voice.

His brows lifted. 'You can pay lip service to

your pride if you want, but it's not *your* life we are talking about, is it?'

She flushed at the quiet reprimand. 'We have a more than adequate health service.'

It was irrational to be irritated by her attitude considering his entire plan rested on her stubborn pride.

'True, but it is also overstretched. Taking your brother out of that system would free up a bed and cash to allow another person to be treated.'

'One who doesn't have a charitable benefactor? Thanks but no, thanks.' She shook her head and looked at him coldly. 'We pay our way and we don't accept charity.'

'Then don't call it charity, or are you willing to put your pride ahead of your brother's well-being?' *And now who is being manipulative, Seb?*

Close on her brother's accusation his comment really stung. Mari swallowed, suddenly struggling to force the words past the aching occlusion in her throat. She wouldn't cry, not now, not in front of this man.

'Call it a loan.'

Mari's hope flared and died; she had seen the figures in the glossy brochure. 'We would never be able to pay it back.' But could she really sit back and watch her brother struggle back to health when she could have made it so much easier?

He angled a dark brow. 'I got the impression that your brother has an entirely more pragmatic attitude than you…towards *charity*? I could have been wrong…?'

He wasn't, damn him. If she refused this offer Mark would never forgive her, and if she took it she would never be able to live with herself.

It was a lose-lose situation.

'Why didn't you just make this offer to him? Why did you have to bring me into it at all?'

'I wanted to see if you are as stubborn and proud as I thought you were—you are.'

'So this is some sort of twisted test? Presumably I failed so now you punish both of—'

His voice was gravelled with irritation as he cut across her. 'I have no desire for revenge on your brother, and unlike you I don't think collateral damage is legitimate.' He allowed her guilty flush to develop before finishing softly, 'If I want to punish you I will.'

Looking into the mirrored surface of his dark eyes, Mari had no problem believing him.

'So you're saying that you do want revenge on me.' She held a tight grip on her bravado and fought off the effects of the apprehensive shiver that slid its clammy way down her spine.

It would take a very dim person not to realise being the target of this man's revenge would not be comfortable.

'If I did I'd be stupid to warn you, wouldn't I?'

Or very clever. All manner of convoluted double bluffs ran through her mind until she felt not just apprehensive but dizzy!

The rain had begun to fall in earnest. In moments the face turned up to him was wet, a perfect classic oval. The moisture glistening on her pale skin highlighted the freckles across the bridge of her small straight nose and the bluish smudges under her beautiful accusing eyes. She looked delicate, sexy and vulnerable.

The sharp, strong stab of something that came perilously close to tenderness was mitigated by an equally strong slug of more familiar lust that pierced him as his gaze fastened on her shirt, where the buttons were straining against her heaving breasts. The rain that was falling heavier now had drenched the fabric, and he could see the scalloped edge of her bra against her breasts.

She really did have an incredible body, he thought, aiming for objectivity as his appreciative gaze slid over her feminine silhouette. Not hourglass—although her waist was tiny, the flare of her hips was less extravagant and her firm high bottom was taut rather than full, mak-

ing her long-legged frame athletic rather than
overtly lush.

And very, very sexy.

His analysis fell way short of objective. He
found her body as provocative as her confron-
tational attitude. The combination was... He
struggled to find the right word. *Stimulating*
was a reasonable approximation and one that a
man who liked boundaries, who needed control,
could live with.

It was ridiculous that he was allowing himself
to be distracted by sex like some hormone-laden
teenager, when there were much more important issues at stake. For a time over the weekend it had seemed as if the royal deal was dead
in the water; it still might be if this went the
wrong way.

'We need to move on.'

'Where?'

His expressive lips twisted in irritation. 'Let's
consider the matter closed. I have made contact
with the clinic and it is all settled. Your brother
is being transferred tomorrow and there is no
reason he should know who is footing the bill
if that is the way you want it.'

Presented with this fait accompli, Mari shook
her head in disbelief, the only response she felt
capable of giving. The tension that had sprung
up seemingly from nowhere hung heavy in the

damp air, and breathing had become something that required conscious effort. It was, she thought guiltily, a sad commentary on her as a sister that she remained so vulnerable to the sexual charge that this man emanated. He didn't even have to try... *What would happen if he did try?*

She pushed the question away, unwilling and unable to deal with the distraction or for that matter the answer it might produce.

The silence that built seemed to have a life of its own and a heartbeat that she could feel pulsing. Her fingers plucked fretfully at the knot of bright fabric at the base of her throat until she blurted with more force than she intended, 'I don't want you in our life!'

Well, that came from the heart, he thought, directing a slow, sardonic, mirthless smile her way. 'You should have thought of that before you put yourself in mine.'

She shivered. It was a comment she felt in whole-hearted agreement with; she was living with the consequences of her own actions. The knowledge did not make it easier.

'Why would you help my brother if you don't think you're responsible? You expect me to believe that you're some sort of altruistic saint?'

His rebuttal was immediate. 'My offer is not inspired by guilt.' Not his guilt, but his tenderhearted sister was showing a tendency to beat herself up about things, and if her ex-boyfriend ended up in a wheelchair that situation would not improve. He would do everything in his power to make sure that didn't happen.

Mari remained suspicious of this very expensively packaged gift horse. Though in the equine world, of course, he would be a thoroughbred, sleek and muscled— With a tiny shake of her head she closed down the thought. 'So what do I have to do? What's the catch?'

'There is no catch, no strings. As I said, I have already spoken to the clinic and your brother will be transferred tomorrow once the paperwork is done. My lawyer will send you the details of an account I have set up in your name for the purpose. I think the funds are adequate, but if there is not enough you simply have to let him know. As I said, it is up to you what you tell your brother. If you'd prefer he remains in ignorance from where the money is coming that is no problem.'

'*I* will know!' Mari always paid her debts— how was she going to pay this one? Submerged by a massive wave of sheer helplessness, she lifted her face to the leaden sky, letting the rain wash over her face.

Seb dragged a hand through his drenched hair

and gave a grunt of irritation; the rain was now drumming on the roof of the car.

'This is ridiculous.' He wrenched open the car passenger door and walked around to the driver's side, yelling over to the slim figure who had made no effort to take advantage of the shelter, 'Personally I've nothing against the wet-shirt look, but...'

She glanced down and let out a horrified gasp.

A moment after he had slammed the door she slid into the passenger seat and sat there staring straight ahead, her arms folded across her chest.

A grin split the severity of his lean features. 'Very modest, but you see a hell of a lot more on a beach.'

She lowered her hands defiantly. 'I'm not embarrassed,' she lied. 'I'm cold.'

He let his eyes drop. 'I'd noticed.'

Longing to slap the lopsided grin off his too-handsome face, she balled her hands into fists. 'Smutty schoolboy innuendo. I'd sort of expected something a bit more...'

The grin faded and it was replaced by something far more dangerous, far *more*... She felt her insides quiver helplessly in response to that nameless *thing*.

'Is that a request?' he asked smokily.

On the brink of succumbing to the heat of his hypnotic stare, her blue eyes flew wide open. It was definitely time to change the subject or at least remember what it was!

'No, not…' *Definitely not.*

'So no work today?' he asked casually.

Suspicious of his sudden question, she shook her head. 'No.'

'One of those consequences you didn't consider?'

Mari maintained a tight-lipped silence.

'I can't imagine that exclusive school you work for liking the idea of its employees' sex scandals being made public.'

Bristling with suspicion, she turned in her seat. 'How do you know what I do or where I work? Have you had my phone bugged or something?' It was as likely as any of the other wild, nausea-inducing possibilities whirling through her head.

'That would be illegal.'

She gave a scornful snort. 'And you have never broken a rule.' Rules and a thousand hearts, she thought, glad that she was not the sort of woman who had ever had a thing for bad boys.

'I have my resources.'

Seb's *resource* in this instance had been the family lawyer who had witnessed firsthand the wedding drama. It had been the one call that Seb had taken on Saturday night, assuming, wrongly as it happened, that it concerned the possible legal ramifications of the incident.

'I had no idea you even knew Miss Jones, Sebastian. Let alone—!'

The lawyer whose services he had inherited when his grandfather died had sounded as unhappy as Seb had ever heard him, a situation brought about not by any sense of indignation for his client but the disruption to his granddaughter's schooling.

'You do know she's the first teacher that has understood Gwennie? The child actually *wants* to go to school and you know what that place is like—they justify their ridiculous fees by claiming they provide a wholesome learning environment, and they have a very good reputation. Hypocrisy, I know, but from a business standpoint they can't afford a sniff of anything…*sexual*, not with the sort of parent the place attracts. The best the poor girl can hope for is suspension after this gets out.'

Listening to the woman who had lied through her teeth, sabotaged his marriage, dragged his reputation into the gutter and in the process endangered the deal he had worked so hard to pull off being spoken of as a victim, described as *poor*, had been as hard for Seb to swallow as visualising the red-headed virago as an empathic teacher.

Would she be as empathic in the bedroom?

'Your resources?' His cryptic comment sent a shiver through her. 'Well, that sounds suitably sinister.'

She gave a laugh, which missed 'bring it on, I don't care' by several thousand miles. Nonetheless, he picked up on it.

'But you're not about to be intimidated.' Seb felt a fresh stab of reluctant admiration; whatever else she was this woman was not gutless. Right or wrong—actually *wrong*—she had gone out on a very precarious limb to fight for her brother, and, having met the guy again, he doubted that he appreciated how lucky he was to have someone like her in his corner.

If the situation had been reversed would Mark Jones have put himself on the line for his sister? Seb doubted it. Nothing he had seen had given him any reason to alter his initial assessment of Mari's twin.

Mari ignored the comment.

'I have spoken to the head, and he was very understanding,' she retorted, putting a positive slant on a situation that when she allowed herself to think about it looked very black indeed.

'But you're not in work today? He was not *that* understanding?'

She slung him a look of seething dislike. 'All right, you were right. My life is a mess, people who I've never met are discussing surgery I never had and it's my own fault.' Which of course made it worse. 'I achieved nothing and now I'm likely to lose my job, too.'

She closed her eyes, feeling herself falling into the relentless cycle of self-recriminating circles that she had spent the entire weekend trying to escape.

'Self-pity doesn't suit you.'

She opened her eyes with an outraged snap and snarled, 'Go to hell!' Then she closed them again.

Her moment of madness still seemed unreal; when she thought of it now it felt like some sort of out-of-body experience.

It made no sense. It wasn't as if she hadn't been painfully aware of the dangers of reacting in the heat of the moment—two foster families had felt unable to cope with the twins after she had *reacted*.

It was a lesson Mari had learned well. In the short term there was immense satisfaction in making the boy who stole your brother's lunch money cry and walloping the bully who shut a puppy in a telephone kiosk—the black eye had been so worth it—but there were consequences.

There always were, which was why she no longer reacted before she thought—she considered consequences to the point where Mark frequently complained about her lack of spontaneity. But on Saturday she'd not just been spontaneous, she'd been… She shuddered and shook her head, bringing her chin up. She'd done the crime so now it was about taking the punishment—whatever that might be…

'I know of a job vacancy that might suit you.'

She opened her eyes and turned her head, still nestled on the leather headrest, to face him, not bothering to hide her suspicion. 'You suddenly became Santa Claus?'

'No, I suddenly became in need of a wife.'

She struggled to match his flippancy. 'Is that a proposal?'

'Yes.'

The colour flared hot and then faded pale in her cheeks as she sat bolt upright and reached for the door handle. 'I'm assuming this is some sort of joke. Word to the wise—don't give up your day job. Stand-up is *not* your thing.'

'What I am suggesting is a business arrangement.' Only his long fingers silently drumming on the steering wheel suggested he was not as relaxed as he appeared.

Mari's fingers tightened on the handle. 'Hate is not a good basis for a business arrangement.'

'I've factored that in,' he retorted with unimpaired cool. 'In public we would act the happy, loved-up couple.'

A hissing sound left her lips. 'Marriage. You're *actually* talking about *marriage*—it's not a sick joke?' She scanned his face. 'What planet do you live on?'

'In private you can carry on hating me and to a large extent living your own life. Eighteen months, we decided, would suffice before we make our irreconcilable differences public—'

'We...?' Listening now simply because she couldn't believe what he was saying, not because she was for one second buying into his crazy suggestion, she pulled the door she had opened closed with a loud, angry bang that shook the car. 'What is this—proposal by committee?'

Every little girl's dream, Mari thought, repressing a sudden strong impulse to laugh, or was that cry?

'I've had my legal people draw up a contract. It's ready for your lawyer to look at.'

He spoke as if everyone had a legal team waiting at the end of the phone. 'I don't have a lawyer. You'd be surprised by how many people in the real world don't.'

He ignored her sarcasm. 'I suggest you get one before you sign up for this.'

Mari took a deep breath. She had humoured him too long. 'I'm not going to sign up for *this*— you're mad,' she said with total conviction. 'Why the hell would you want to get married? Assuming that you haven't decided I'm your soulmate.'

'This is about damage limitation, not soulmates,' he cut back, ignoring her sarcasm. 'I have spent the weekend trying to repair the damage your stunt inflicted on a crucial business deal.'

His comment stirred a memory. 'The royal thing?'

He tipped his head in acknowledgement. 'Good, you know about it, so I don't have to explain that the royal family are very nervous about scandal, *especially* the sexual kind that involves men getting women pregnant and deserting them.'

'So you told them you didn't know me.'

An expression she could not quite read flickered across his face as he looked at her. 'Strangely, you know, I feel I do, but no, the truth would not have worked. You were way too convincing, angel. I almost believed you myself except I think I might have remembered sleeping with you. No, this was a situation that required some creativity.'

'Lies, you mean. Like the one when you said there were no strings to you paying for Mark's treatment!'

'No, I meant that if you refuse my proposal

your brother's treatment will still be funded. The two are not co-dependent.'

'So why would I say yes without blackmail?'

'Because you don't want to be in my debt...' His narrow-eyed scrutiny moved across her face. 'The idea of that kills you, doesn't it?' This thing hung on her stiff-necked pride and his ability to keep his lust in check. This needed to stay business and he needed to retain control.

'Yes!' she flung back, hating him so much she could taste it.

'Excellent... In that case you should probably know about us.'

'About...?'

'I gave us a history. We had a short passionate relationship, but there was a lovers' falling-out—we can't even remember what the fight was about now. We met up again not long ago by accident, we shared a night of passion, but we were both with other people by then and we went our separate ways. I had no idea you were pregnant until you appeared. Seeing you again has made me realise that you are the love of my life.'

It was all delivered in the sort of deadpan tone that made a computerised voice sound animated. Mari looked at him, fascinated. 'And they swallowed that?'

'I lack your dramatic talent,' he admitted drily. 'There was no soul baring involved. The reality is they have as much time and money invested in this deal as I do and they are less concerned about me doing the right thing than me being *seen* to do the right thing.'

'They sound as shallow as you.'

'It's called realism. You ought to try it some time.'

'I can see a massive flaw in your plan—the baby—so do you expect me to walk around with a pillow shoved down my jumper, too?'

'That won't be necessary. We will be away on an extended honeymoon when you tragically lose the baby. It's not something we want to talk about and people will respect that.'

'You've thought of everything.'

'If not, I'm pretty good at thinking on my feet.'

'And modest with it,' she snapped back waspishly.

'So what do you say, Mari Jones? Eighteen months of your life, then afterwards slate clean and a financial settlement to ease your way back into your life? It's negotiable but the figure I suggest is—'

'No!'

He watched as she chewed her plump lip, an abstracted expression on her face, before she settled back in her seat with a little sigh followed by a decisive nod as she looked at him.

'Make it *exactly* what Mark's treatment costs and you have a deal.' She gave him a hard look.

'That would amount to you throwing away several million pounds.'

'I don't care about the money.'

'I assumed you would go away and think about it.'

She gave a slightly wild-sounding laugh. 'Thinking is the last thing I want to do! The only thing is…when you said this was business you wouldn't expect me to—'

'I have never had to pay for sex.'

His eyes trained on the outline of her breasts where the nipples left an erotic imprint against the wet fabric of her shirt. Unable to fight the impulse, he reached across and pushed aside a strand of rain-darkened hair that clung to her cheek.

The touch of his fingers on her skin made Mari tense; slowly she turned her head to look at him. The light contact felt like a brand at every point of contact and her skin tingled and burned.

'Right, I'll marry you but I won't sleep with you.'

A slow smile of satisfaction spread across his hawkish features. 'In my experience it's always a good idea to keep business and pleasure separate, but let's not include it in the vows.'

Mari flinched. Hearing him say *vows* made it

seem more real. She felt as if she were living a recurrent childish nightmare of hers—she had stepped on a carousel that wouldn't stop and let her off, it just carried on going round and round while she started screaming.

His smile died as he said softly, 'The next time maybe…?'

She gave a bemused frown and shook her head, parroting in a flat voice, 'Next time?'

'Don't all girls dream of the wedding dress?'

'Not the groom?'

'Let's hope you find a man who hasn't been put off the white-wedding thing by having been previously publicly humiliated by a wedding crasher. Oh, and while we are on the subject it's not the best idea to start looking for Mr. Right or even a little light entertainment until *after* we have split up.'

Struggling to hide her embarrassment behind an air of amused indifference, she shrugged and asked, 'Is that in the small print?'

He did not smile back, and there was a definite warning in his voice as he told her, 'No, that part is in the *big* print. If it's any comfort, you won't be the only one condemned to eighteen months of celibacy.'

What was eighteen months when you'd already done twenty-four years? she thought, swallowing the bubble of hysteria that rose in her throat.

'Still, I suppose eighteen months of abstinence is preferable to a lifetime of regret.'

She lost the battle to allow his cynicism go unchallenged. 'I suppose the trick is to find the right person.'

He gave an eloquent sneer of contempt. 'The trick is to enjoy the party but be realistic.'

His attitude continued to get under Mari's skin. 'So if you don't believe people fall in love forever, why were you getting married?'

A muscle throbbed in his lean cheek as he gave a strange twisted smile. 'Did I say I didn't think people fall in love forever? My parents' passion for one another is as strong today, I would think, as the day they met.' And just as blindly selfish.

The idea of following their example had been the perfect incentive when it came to keeping his own passions under control.

She was bewildered by the aura of anger he was projecting. It had an almost physical presence in the enclosed space.

'Well, that's marvellous.' She looked at him, struggling to read his expression. *Isn't it?*

'My parents' *love* has not stopped them having affairs, but they always come back to one another. However the divorces were never amicable and the marriages always headline-making lavish.'

Her eyes widened. 'How many times?'

'Married three times, divorced twice…so far.'

'That must have been hard growing up.'

The tentative sympathy was met with a hard look. 'Put your empathy away, Mari. I do not need it. My grandfather brought me over from the Argentine to England when I was eight, up from that point he raised me, and then when Fleur came along he adopted her.'

'Do you spend much time in Argentina?'

He shook his head. 'Not now. After the death of her husband my grandmother moved back to her homeland, Spain. I spend some time there.' He handed her a card. 'My private number—ring me if you have any questions. So where shall I take you?'

'I came in my own car,' she said faintly. 'So what happens…now?'

'We get married. It's not complicated.'

Mari swallowed. 'When?'

'I'll be in touch.'

CHAPTER SIX

MARI WAS PACKING her bag when her mobile rang. Finding it under a pile of underclothes, she saw the caller ID and picked it up. Chloe had been her classroom assistant for two years now. She was one of the people Mari would miss most, along with the children. She had always felt she was one of the lucky ones. She loved her job and never woke up not wanting to go into work—now all that was gone.

She pushed the thought away—no time to look back and have regrets. 'Hi, Chloe!'

'Is it true? Have they really sacked you?' Without waiting for a reply the girl continued indignantly, 'Is that even legal?'

'I'm on a temporary contract. It runs out at the end of the term.' Not long ago there had been some pretty broad hints dropped that she might be offered a permanent contract at that point, but that was not going to happen now.

'They are giving me paid leave until then and a good reference.'

Would Sebastian give her a good reference when their contract was successfully completed? She swallowed a bubble of hysteria and heard the younger girl say, 'Well, I think it's terrible. We all do, Mari—you're the best teacher in the place.'

Mari felt her eyes fill at the tribute.

'So what are you going to do?'

'I thought I might travel a bit, take a trip.' She kept it vague, as she had done the previous day when she had visited Mark, though Chloe showed a lot more interest in her plans than her brother had.

Mark had barely listened when she'd said that she needed to take a trip. All he could talk about were the arrangements for his transfer— his mention of her part in the change in his fortune had been lightly touched on.

'I knew if you could swallow your pride it would be all right. I've no idea what you said to him, sis, but it worked, Seb has done the right thing.'

'I didn't say anything. How do you know it was him?'

'Who else would it be? And don't look like that.' He'd sighed. 'You always managed to ruin things with that guilt thing of yours. It's win-

win—he can go around feeling good because he's dug his hand in his pocket for the poor cripple and, let's face it, it's not as though he doesn't owe me. He put me here after all.'

Did he…? Mari's innate honesty could no longer support the deception. She felt guilty for not being more sympathetic to her brother, and when the opportunity arose she'd leaped at the chance to offload that guilt onto someone else.

'I knew you'd come through for me, sis—you always do.'

When his eyes slid from hers she realised that he didn't want to know how. Her twin always had a knack to ignore uncomfortable truths, the ones that made him uncomfortable anyway.

It was an ability Mari envied him.

She was expecting the knock on the door but she jumped anyway.

She'd been expecting a flunkey of some sort, so when she opened the door and found Seb himself standing there she was too shocked to disguise her reaction. Her jaw dropped and her blue eyes flew wide open. The raw masculinity he exuded hit her like a runaway train.

Like someone coming out of a trance, she blinked and hoped her knees would support her. 'What are you doing here?' It came out a lot more accusingly than she had intended.

In response his dark brows lifted as without a word he stepped past her and into the living room. He subjected the long narrow space to the same sort of critical scrutiny that she'd endured, and from his expression she assumed it had been assessed as wanting, also.

Lucky she didn't crave his approval. In fact she told herself if the day ever dawned that she got it, that was the time to worry.

'I said one o'clock. It is one.' His frown deepened. 'Aren't you ready?'

Trying not to react to his abrupt manner, she gave a curt nod, and, matching his noticeably cold attitude, indicated her bag propped up against the sofa, one of several pieces of furniture in the place she had reupholstered or revamped. She couldn't sew a stitch, but she was a whiz with a staple gun and a paintbrush.

'Of course I'm ready.' Was this about the way she looked? 'Should I go back and put on my tiara?' She tried to hide a sudden flash of uncharacteristic insecurity under sarcasm.

He slung her an impatient look. 'What are you talking about?'

'I thought, you thought that I…maybe should, should I wear something a bit more…?' She glanced down at her slim-fitting jeans and the cropped jacket left open to reveal the silky acid-yellow sleeveless top that showed a tiny sliver of flat midriff.

His eyes moved in an expressionless sweep from her toes to the top of her glossy head. 'You look fine. It's only a register office.'

Wow, he sure knows how to make a girl feel good, she thought, compressing her lips in silent resentment, furious with herself for virtually asking for his approval.

'Actually I wasn't expecting you. I assumed you'd send a driver or something.'

Her calm was only a single cell thick, but it was very important to Mari that he had no idea just how *not* calm she was. She was almost sick with apprehension, and under that there were layers of confusing, conflicting emotions that were just too complicated to acknowledge. On a more practical level she was worried she might actually throw up.

'So how long will it take...?'

He dragged his gaze from that tiny sliver of flat, toned, creamy-skinned stomach and cleared his throat, reminding himself that this was business.

'The flight or—?'

'Both,' she cut in quickly.

'The company jet was available, so not long for the journey. The wedding I've arranged so that we can stop off on the way to the airport.'

'That sounds ideal.' Her voice was clear and cool but Seb could see her hands were shaking as her gaze flickered around the room; she was looking anywhere but at him. She reminded him of a trapped animal.

She accused him of pride, but Seb suspected that Mari's stiff-necked version of that sin would make her walk over hot coals before she'd admit she was nervous. It was an exasperating characteristic, almost as much as her wildly misplaced loyalty to her brother and he was not above exploiting this misplaced loyalty.

Which makes you...?

She was a consenting adult; she knew what she was doing. Somehow this didn't stop his pangs of conscience.

'It's all right to be nervous.'

'I'm not nervous. I'll just be glad when it's over.'

'Is this all you have?' He nodded towards the moderate-size holdall that was propped against a sofa that had *bespoke* and *expensive* written all over it. The open-plan living area suggested that the owner had expensive taste.

'I fit a lot in. I wasn't sure what to bring.' She hurried and clumsily snatched the bag up before him. 'I can manage,' she said with the attitude of someone expecting a fight.

No fight materialised; he simply straight-

ened up and watched as she flung it purpose-
fully over her shoulder, allowing himself a faint
smile when the impetus as it hit her hip almost
knocked her off balance.

'Fine by me.'

'That's good, then,' she said, knowing the response sounded lame.

Mari lived on the fourth floor in a small non-
descript brick building that had no lift, and by
the time they had reached the third floor she was
regretting he hadn't argued her out of her decision. Halfway down she swallowed her pride
and paused to catch her breath.

He paused, too, not breathless obviously, just
looking like a Hollywood film star who had
drifted onto the wrong set. This peeling paint
and worn carpet really wasn't his natural setting.

He looked down at her through the mesh of
his crazily long dark eyelashes and nodded to
the bag. 'Manage that, can you?'

She gritted her teeth, straightened up and pro-
duced a sunny smile. The weight had almost
yanked her shoulder from its socket, but she'd
die before she'd admit it or accept his help. 'I'm
fine, thank you.'

He stood aside as she exited the flat door side-
ways, not making allowances for the bulk of the
bag as she eased past him carefully.

'Sure you don't need help?'

'Yes,' she said shortly, requiring all her breath to negotiate the last flight of stairs. They passed one of her neighbours, whose plucked brows almost vanished into her hairline when she saw Seb.

'Moving on, are we?'

'A holiday,' Mari puffed.

'I don't think she believed you,' Seb said in a voice that echoed spookily down the stairwell.

'Shh, she'll hear you,' Mari hissed as she prepared to swap shoulders, resting her bag for a moment on the step long enough to give him ample opportunity to repeat his offer of help. She'd refuse, but it would be nice to have the option. When he didn't, she gritted her teeth and wished she hadn't packed the books or the pair of boots.

'The reporters knocked on every door in the building. I think they offered money for—'

His lip curled. 'Dirt.'

She turned her head; he was standing two steps behind her.

'I was surprised,' he admitted, stepping down one step and pausing just one above her.

Too close...too close... Struggling to pacify the panicky voice in her head, she took a jolting backward step.

'Really? I thought knocking on doors and buying stories was par for the course?'

'It is, which is why I was surprised when I didn't get to read the lurid details, both fictional and true, of your love affairs in the tabloids. Anyone would think you have a blemish-free past.' The humourless smile that tugged the corners of his mouth upwards faded as his hooded gaze slid covetously over the curves of her athletically slim body. She had an innate sensuality that had to make every man she met think about taking her to bed—he had.

Still was thinking, said the voice in his head.

The difference was he wasn't going to act on it, despite the sizzle whenever they were in near proximity. This might be a long eighteen months.

It didn't matter how hard they dug, she didn't have a past, at least not the sort he was talking about, but Mari was not about to admit her embarrassing lack of lovers to him. She turned her head quickly. Trust issues aside, she had suspected for some time that she simply wasn't very highly sexed. With Adrian she had been in love with the idea of it, the romance of it, which was why having her illusions shattered had been such a big deal.

She'd trusted him and he'd betrayed her and rejected her. She'd prefer to stay single than risk feeling that way again.

'Some of us are discreet.'

'Yeah, I had a grandstand view of your *amazing* discretion in the cathedral,' he drawled, replaying the scene in his head and feeling the acrid aftertaste of anger and humiliation all over again.

Mari clamped her lips together. She was pretty sick of having her nose rubbed in it. It wasn't as if she needed reminding she had set in motion the events that had led her to this place and this moment. 'Are you going to bring that up often? Just so that I know.'

'You're right.' Anger was a waste of energy and an indulgence; he needed to take a less negative approach. 'I'm not in the best of moods.'

Astonished by the admission, Mari didn't say anything.

'After a long absence, my parents have made the news.'

The story dug up from years back by an enterprising hack told of another bride left standing at the altar. His father had been the groom, his mother the 'other' woman, and his father had jilted his new bride just as Seb had done.

The only downside to this story from a journalistic point of view had been that the woman left at the altar had not gone on to lead a tragic life, but instead had been inconveniently happy combining a career as a respected trauma doctor with marriage and four children.

'Today might be better if you remind yourself that a marriage of convenience is a hell of a lot better than one of inconvenience, and there are a lot of those out there,' he mused, fighting the impulse to grab the damned bag off her as she staggered awkwardly down a step. All she had to do was ask, but she didn't, and with a bloody-minded stubbornness she made it to the poky communal hallway where she paused.

He correctly interpreted her hesitation. 'There were no reporters outside when I arrived.'

Still she hesitated, raising herself up on tip-toe to peer through the dusty pane of glass high up on the door.

'Are you sure?' If she was seen leaving complete with luggage and Seb, she could only imagine how they would spin it. Ironically nothing could be as strange, or crazy, as the truth!

With a grunt of irritation he snatched the bag from her and strode out through the door.

Left with little choice Mari followed him, relieved that no one jumped out of the shadows wielding a camera. He walked straight to the car parked by the kerb. It was an enormous four-wheel drive with blacked-out windows.

'You're driving?'

'I like driving, unless you want to?'

She shook her head.

'So what did your brother think of our arrangement?' Being a brother himself, his opinion of a man who allowed his sister to fight his battles was not positive.

'I don't ask my brother's approval for my decisions.'

Neatly dodged, he thought, observing her neat, peachy behind as she bent, ignoring the passenger door and getting into the back seat.

'Aren't you going to ask me where we're going?'

She had been about to, but she responded to a perverse impulse and said instead, 'One register office is much the same as any other.'

She saw his eyes narrow in the rear-view mirror. 'Life is going to be a lot easier if you lose the victim act,' he drawled.

Not replying, she turned her head and looked out of the window.

'The silent treatment works for me. It's peaceful, but I've never known a woman who can keep it buttoned for more than five minutes.'

Mari clamped her lips over a retort and contented herself with slinging him a fulminating look of dislike in the rear-view mirror.

'Fifteen, I'm impressed,' Seb admitted as he drew up in front of a red-brick building.

She ignored him and looked up at the building. 'So this is it, then?'

He glanced over his shoulder. 'We're five minutes early. I can drive around the block once more if you like?' he suggested, fighting the impulse to apologise.

It was convenient, but had he realised that the office was situated on a road where most shop windows were either boarded up or smashed, he would have added a few miles to their journey.

Mari shook her head and took a deep breath. Not waiting for him to come around and open the door, she flung herself out, gasping, 'No, I'm fine.'

She had actually never been this far from *fine* in her life!

Seb came to join her. 'It's probably better inside.'

It was actually much worse, but Mari barely noticed. It wasn't the place that made her heart feel like a stone; it was exchanging words that were meant to *mean* something. She felt a hypocrite saying them—making a mockery of something that she considered sacred left a bad taste in her mouth.

Mari felt like a cheat.

As they walked through the swing doors, Seb pulled Mari out of the way of a boisterous crowd. At the centre of the laughing group was a bride whose white minidress did nothing to disguise her large pregnancy bump and a groom who didn't look as if he had started shaving yet.

Mari turned her head for one last look as the loud group left the building.

'They looked so happy.'

Seb didn't know if it was the wistful look on her face when she said it, or the fact he had fully expected her to make some catty remark about the other woman giving birth before she got to exchange vows, but as they headed towards the ceremony room Seb found himself wishing he had bought her some flowers.

CHAPTER SEVEN

THE MOMENT MARI got out of the car, even though it was almost midnight, the Spanish summer heat hit her. She focused on the physical impressions and tried not to think beyond them to the lump of apprehension she was carrying around like a stone in her chest for the entire journey.

It was utterly still; the air was heavy and stickily oppressive. For the last mile or so they had driven through what seemed to be a pine forest, and warm air carried the green smell of the trees.

She got out her mobile and texted goodnight to her brother.

'I imagine he is much as he was the past ten times you texted him.' While Seb was exploiting the sisterly devotion, her inability to see that she was being used by her brother was really beginning to irritate him. So was her frigid, tight-lipped silence.

She had not said anything the entire journey;

not to him anyway—she had been charm itself to the steward on the flight. The boy had been positively salivating. 'And you've proved your point. Some women can keep quiet.'

He had hardly said a word the entire way, so now he broke his moody silence to criticise her!

'If you'd spoken to me I'd have replied. And texting my brother, that's called caring,' she snapped back, choosing not to inform him that the texting exercise had been pretty one-sided.

He turned his head briefly to scan her profile in the darkness. 'Would he be grateful if he knew what you've done for him?'

'You're the one who is paying for his treatment. This was my choice.'

'So why didn't you tell him?'

'Mark has got enough on his plate without feeling responsible... What's that meant to mean?' she asked in response to his harsh laugh.

'Is it a happy place, this little fantasy world you inhabit?'

Mari shot a look of simmering dislike at his patrician profile. 'I wouldn't expect you to understand.'

'Try me.'

Taken unawares by the unexpected offer, Mari found herself answering, 'I love him. He's my brother.' She could have left it there but for some reason she heard herself say, 'I know he's not perfect but he's not had an easy life, rejected by his mother.'

'Is that the way you feel about it—rejected?'

Too close to the truth. She ignored his interruption.

'Two foster homes that didn't work out, and the children's home—'

'Weren't you in those same places?'

She shook her head. 'You don't understand—he was there *because* of me. He would have been adopted straight away when we were babies if they had allowed us to be split up, but they didn't.'

'Why him and not you?'

'People want pretty babies. Mark had blond curls and dimples—he was adorable. I was not an attractive baby.' It was a matter-of-fact statement with no self-pity he could detect, and all the more poignant because of it.

'Aren't all babies pretty?'

'Not me. I was allergic to pretty much everything. I had asthma, that wasn't so bad, but my skin was awful—eczema. It took hours every day putting on and washing off my treatments... and when it flared up...' She gave a little shudder at the memory. 'People do not want to push around a scabby baby, and not many want the responsibility of looking after a kid with a chronic skin condition.

'Mark got left on the shelf with me, and when we did get fostered my red-headed temper—well, you've seen that—got us sent back both times. So, you see, without me Mark could have had a very different life.'

'Is that how you think of yourself—left on the shelf…?'

'Actually it was a doorstep.' To abandon your own babies that way you had to be pretty desperate…but maybe if there had only been one…?

She heard him swear and then, anxious that he didn't think she was playing for the sympathy vote, added quickly, 'It wasn't all doom and gloom, though, in our teens. We got fostered by Sukie and Jack, and they are the most inspirational couple you can imagine,' she enthused, her voice filling with warmth.

'Are you coming?'

He knew it was irrational of him to be angry with her for not being a person he could despise. It was a lot easier to take advantage of someone when you could say they were asking for it, they deserved it, than someone who literally didn't ask for anything, and as far as he could see had never been given anything either! Mari had worked hard and…ah, hell, she was an adult. If she wanted to spend her life paying an imagined debt, that was her business, he told himself. The story changed nothing.

Mari began to follow and stopped. He didn't even bother to turn around and see if she'd responded, just assumed she would.

And why wouldn't he? She'd been responding like some meek little lamb from the moment she'd allowed herself to be bundled onto the private jet and, yes, there had been a certain amount of novelty value in the unaccustomed luxury, but it had worn off and now... *What the hell are you doing, Mari?*

Mari Rey-Defoe.

Mrs Rey-Defoe.

She pressed a hand to her lips but the giggle slipped past. She was married. She used both hands this time to muffle the hysteria that was locked in her throat.

From where he was standing, Seb, who had walked halfway across the gravel, heard it. There was irritation written in the lines of his lean face when he turned and saw her still standing near the car. All he could make out was the shadowy outline of her slim figure, then the moon came out from behind the heavy cloud cover.

He swore softly under his breath. Nothing, he thought savagely, was easy with this woman. She had set out to make his life as tough as possible, and when she couldn't stage something large and dramatic she made do with little niggling details that added up to a massive and frustrating whole.

The logical thing to do would have been to put her out of his life and erect six walls to keep her out, and yet here he was dragging her in and effectively building walls to keep her there for eighteen long months. Eighteen excruciating months without sex, spent with a woman who could make a sneeze erotic.

At what point had this seemed like a logical next step?

It was a means to an end, he reminded himself. This was about saving several thousand jobs and a partnership that in the future could generate a lot more—a means to an end.

Sure it is, the voice in his head mocked, *the end being your bed*.

The illicit thought came with the accompanying image; he had undressed her in his head over the past few days so often that he felt he knew exactly what she would look like.

He ignored the voice and the desire that twisted inside him, and reminded himself this was a business deal. You let business get personal and it never ended well.

'Come on.' The idea of a shower and bed was appealing; the idea of a bed with Mari in it… He saw red hair spread out against the white sheet framing a face that… He clenched his jaw against the thought, but not before his body hardened. 'It's this way. Watch your step.' He jerked his head towards the house.

Ignoring the gesture—did the man think she was some sort of puppy dog to be brought to heel?—Mari shook her head and struggled to maintain her defiant attitude as he crossed the gravel towards her, his long-legged stride bringing him there in seconds.

The resentful words exploded from her before the testosterone he was oozing made her tongue stick to the roof of her mouth, a situation she been experiencing all day.

'You've been pushing me around all day.'

Not in the literal sense. It had almost seemed at times as though he had gone out of his way to avoid touching her. Even at the joke of a marriage ceremony when the registrar had said he could kiss the bride, Seb had barely even brushed his lips with hers, leaving her looking and feeling like a total fool.

The aggravating part of the situation was she had been letting him, and it was not a good precedent to set for the next eighteen months with a man as bossy and controlling as Seb.

She folded her arms across her chest. 'I've had enough. You're a control freak, and I'm not going another step until you tell me where we are.'

'Don't be childish. All you had to do was ask,

but you were too busy playing the victim and giving me the stink eye.'

'I'm amazed you noticed. You haven't looked up from that damned tablet the whole way.'

'Feeling neglected, were we?'

'Not at all,' she retorted haughtily. 'It was an education to see what delightful manners years of inbreeding and the best school can achieve.' It had gone pitch-black again, but his answering hiss made her decide to move on. She'd made her point, although she'd forgotten what it was as he'd taken a step towards her, not touching but awfully close…too close. 'I'm asking now.'

Now that he was close to losing his temper she sounded maddeningly calm. She had accused him of bad manners, yet she had responded to any question with a mutter and barely said a word the entire way here; filthy looks and her ramrod-straight back—he doubted her shoulder blades had made contact with a chair back at any point—were all that had been given him.

'Fine, but indoors.' He glanced up as a cloud drifted like smoke across the moon. 'There's a storm coming.'

'And you can tell that how?'

Before she could pour further scorn on his confident prediction there was a distant roll of thunder. So instead she flung him a disgruntled glare and directed her gaze at the sinister outline of the stone building they stood before. It rose out of the forest, making her think of a haunted mansion in a Gothic romance. Did that make her the spunky but vulnerable heroine...?

She almost laughed at the thought. She was none of the above!

'I think I'd feel safer out here. There is no way that place is a hotel.' The place looked very Gothic, and a little shiver slid a clammy path down her spine.

'No,' he agreed with infuriating placidity. 'It's not.'

'It looks like the set of a vampire movie!'

Despite himself Seb's lips twitched. 'It was a monastery.'

Her voice rose to an indignant squeak. 'You've brought me to a monastery?'

'*Obviously* it is no longer a monastery. It was for a short time, I believe, a school, and now it is my grandmother's home. Her family came from this area of Spain originally and her twin sister still lives close by. After she was widowed she returned here.'

'I don't believe you.'

'I thought you knew all about the special bond between twins, and my grandmother and Aunt Marguerite are identical.'

'You know what I mean—why in God's

name would you bring me to your grandmother's house?'

'Because it is her birthday tomorrow,' he told her calmly. 'She has been unwell, she is my last living grandparent and I promised to see her.' In as much as there had been a female influence after he had come to live in England, the tough, outspoken old lady who took a delight in being awkward had been it.

'Oh, God!' The idea of being dropped into the middle of a family gathering filled Mari with utter horror she didn't even try to disguise. 'Is your entire family here?'

What had he been thinking?

What was I *thinking?* She pushed away the rush of panicked rejection and focused on a mental image of Mark in a wheelchair. After a moment her sense of purpose reasserted itself and the panic receded.

Many people coped with disability—one of her friends had lost her sight and gone on to not only marry and have a gorgeous child but win a medal for her country in the International Swimming Championships. She was an inspiration, but Mark… No, her brother would not react well.

And how, she wondered, was Sebastian's family going to react to her? How was he going to explain the presence of this new wife? God, but that sounded so weird to think. Would she ever be able to say it out loud?

'No, they aren't here.'

'That's something, I suppose.' Before he stepped back into the shadow there was something in his face that made her probe. 'But they, your mum and dad, I mean, they were at the wedding?' And presumably had filled Granny in on the scandalous proceedings, and just when she thought the situation could not get weirder or more awkward.

'My parents are presently enjoying a world cruise. They were not at my wedding and will not be here.'

The undercurrent in his voice made her say, 'I'm sorry.'

He flicked her a look, opened his mouth and closed it again. She was lifting her shoulders and rolling them to stretch the kinks that tied up her spine after the journey. Seb was struck by the almost feline quality in the sinuous way she moved. He took a deep breath as heat seared through his body, as merciless as a blade. Then he launched into a response designed to dampen her empathy.

'My grandparents on both sides played a larger part in my life than my parents.' He clenched his jaw and taunted softly, 'Aren't you going to say, well, at least you *had* parents?'

'I had parents. Everyone does. The difference is I could walk past them in the street and not know them. They wouldn't know me. I look sometimes and wonder if… When I was little I told people my dad was a war hero and my mother was a nurse.' She stopped, hit by the sheer strangeness and odd intimacy of this encounter, standing in the dark with this man—a man she barely knew but was married to, a man who she had considered her enemy before she knew his name—talking about families.

A subject she knew little of, she thought, ignoring the knot of longing in her chest so familiar she barely acknowledged its presence. She had Mark and he had her; they were a family. Her mother and her reasons for deserting them, which she had trained herself not to think about…*mostly.*

It seemed like a long time before he responded. His voice coming out of the darkness made her jump. 'You stopped.'

'The teacher found out and made me apologise to the class for lying.'

'Sensitive soul. I hope you are a better teacher.'

'I am.' It was not a subject she had any false modesty on. She'd be a better parent, too, than his, who had better things to do than attend their son's wedding.

When her children, the ones Mari dreamed of

one day adopting, had their red-letter days she would be there with bells on!

She tilted her head back, squinting, just able to make out the shape of the tiled roof.

'I can't imagine anyone, let alone an elderly lady, choosing to live here.' Unsure if he had even heard her, she followed the sound of his crunching footsteps because if she lost him she didn't have a clue where she was going.

When he responded Seb's deep vibrant voice came from a little way ahead. 'It is a lot less intimidating in daylight when the bats are asleep.'

Trotting in earnest to catch up, she fought the urge to duck and cover her head. 'That's a joke, right…?'

'Bats are perfectly harmless creatures, more frightened of you than you are of them.'

'Want to bet?'

His low laugh was so attractive that she had to fight a responsive grin. She had to fight a few other responses, too. She was familiar with the notion that opposites attracted and that sexual attraction was indiscriminate, but this was her first real experience of how overwhelming it could be when you encountered the sort of intense physical magnetism that Seb possessed. It made what she had felt for Adrian pale into insignificance.

If he had any redeeming features beyond a

fondness for his grandmother she might have been in danger of making a fool of herself and maybe enjoying it, because there was no doubt in her mind that he'd be a good lover. His hands, she mused dreamily, his mouth… Her stomach flipped.

'You can relax.'

Shocked by the direction of her thoughts, Mari realised that was one thing she couldn't do, not around this man with his powerful aura of masculinity.

'My grandmother's home is actually quite civilised, and she is a very young eighty-two. Obviously she doesn't live here alone—a couple live in and there is a gardener and a couple of maids who come in from the village.'

'Cosy set-up,' she murmured, staring at the looming building and not really caring if he got her sarcasm or not, just glad he had no inkling of her previous thoughts. 'I didn't see any village on the way.' Even with her having taken the precaution of turning her back to him, his nearness made the nape of her neck tingle.

'There are two accesses to the place. We took the north road—the village is on the south side of the mountain.'

The geography of the area made little sense to Mari, and her thoughts turned to her brother.

What if something had happened? He hadn't replied to her last text.

She slipped her phone out of her pocket, but before she could begin to punch in Mark's number it was snatched from her grasp by Seb before she had even registered his presence.

She turned, eyes blazing. 'Give that back!'

Seb looked at the phone and tucked it into his own pocket. Mari, her hands clenched, watched him and went white with rage. 'Does he always need you to hold his hand?'

Her chin lifted in reaction to the scorn in his voice while in the distance the owl called. 'The support is mutual.'

A slug of anger that on one level Seb knew was irrational slipped past the cool objectivity he struggled to maintain whenever he thought of the man he had judged to be a selfish waste of space. Any sympathy he might have felt for the younger man's present situation was negated by the cynical way he used his sister and played on her irrational guilt.

And you're not...?

Cynical, or using her?

Both. The answer came a second before he closed down this line of internal dialogue.

The situations were not comparable; she was not losing out and this was a fair exchange. Eighteen months with him was preferable to a life spent looking after a brother for whom nothing she ever did would be enough—and that was what would happen if he didn't fully recover.

Recognising a masterful piece of rationalisation when he heard one, he buried the knowledge beneath a layer of anger.

'You'd like to believe that, wouldn't you? But you're really not that stupid, are you, Mari?'

Mari was grateful for the dark when his soft suggestion made her face flame. She compressed her lips over a defensive retort, resenting his insinuation while recognising there was more than a grain of truth in it. While she wasn't blind to her twin's faults, it was something else to hear another person criticise him.

'Didn't you read the literature on The Atler?'

Her face was just a blur, but he imagined her teeth gouging into the soft plump fullness of her lower lip. She'd done that several times on the plane. At one point there had been pinpricks of blood, and he had wondered what she would do if he'd dabbed them away with his tongue...

The question still remained, as did the frustrated ache.

She was grateful for the change of subject, but it took Mari a moment to react to the abrupt question, to connect the name with the clinic that specialised in the rehabilitation of injuries like Mark's—the *expensive* clinic.

She felt resentment she was uncomfortable acknowledging stir. If she had told Mark what she was doing would he have discouraged her? Her resentment was directed not towards her brother but towards the man who had made her think about it.

'I didn't know there was an exam,' she countered, unwilling to admit that she had read the first page half a dozen times before she had finally given up. She'd had other things on her mind at the time, such as getting married.

Seb, drawn by the scent of her perfume—or was it her shampoo?—fought the sudden strong impulse to lean in closer. Darkness had a dangerous way of bypassing inhibitions.

The air was heavy with an almost audible expectant hum that had little to do with the imminent storm and everything to do with the indiscriminate flare of hormones that escalated the dull ache in his groin.

Sex was always one of those things that defied logic, but not, he reminded himself, his control. He was justifiably proud of his ability to vanquish the primal urges.

'They discourage visitors during the initial

assessment period. The regime appears to be as much boot camp as high-tech.'

'It does?'

'When the going gets tough your brother will be begging you to get him out of there…and of course you'll rush to do what he wants, even if that isn't the best thing for him. If you're here with me, you have a legitimate excuse to refuse to ride to the rescue.'

His superior dismissive tone hit a raw nerve. Mari caught his arm and felt the hard muscle under her fingers tense before he swung back his feet, kicking up a shower of gravel that hit her bare shins.

'You don't think a lot of him, do you?'

His response was not ambiguous. 'No.'

'Because he's not been born with your advantages?' she charged contemptuously. 'Well, my brother has got pride, too, even if he doesn't have the required patrician blood to meet your standards!' She glared up at the shadowy outline of his face.

'I thought pride was a bad and wicked thing. Or is that only when it comes attached to me?'

She was attached to him.

Mari's dark-fringed eyelids fluttered in recognition of the contact; she pulled in a tense breath and felt her insides quiver. At some point her left hand had joined her right on his biceps; she was holding on as though her life depended on it. There was no give at all beneath her fingers. He was hard and lean, strong like steel but warm. She could feel the heat through her fingertips, sending pulses of a dark warmth thrumming through her body.

'Your sort of pride comes from an arrogant belief that you are better simply because you are you. Well, he'll prove you wrong.' Forcing a drop of blood from a stone could not have required more strength than peeling back her strangely reluctant fingers; no matter how hard she tried they wouldn't budge. In the darkness with the wind rustling through the trees her heart began to thud in slow, heavy, hard anticipation.

Of what, Mari?

Time seemed to stop. She struggled, feeling things inside her that had built up begin to dissolve like sand. Control was slipping through her fingers... Shaking her head in rejection, she managed to break the contact and the spell. Holding her hands across her chest in a protective gesture, Mari took a lurching step back onto an uneven cobble and in the process triggered a powerful security light.

Without warning, the area was lit up, revealing that they had entered a courtyard. She lifted a hand to shade her eyes. The scent she had been conscious of was more pronounced, and she saw it emanated from the wild thyme growing in the cracks of the cobbles. The illumination after the anonymity of darkness made her feel exposed and horribly vulnerable.

This was her first real glimpse of the building. Its ecclesiastical origins were obvious in the architecture but the severity was softened by ivy on the walls and massive stone troughs beneath enormous mullioned windows that spilled out their impressive floral displays.

But it was not the geraniums that caught her attention, it was the expression in his eyes. Then the first raindrop hit her face, then another and another. The moment gone, she lifted her face to the heavens with a sigh. If ever a cold shower had been providential, this one was.

'This way,' he said, gesturing for Mari to go ahead of him into a wide, open porch made of oak that had silvered with age. 'Not a creaking door in sight.' He lifted the heavy latch on a massive door just to his right.

'What about bats?'

'Creatures with sharp teeth that launch themselves into the unknown with only instinct to protect them. I would have thought that you would feel something in common with them.'

Stepping under his arm and through the huge door that swung inwards as he lifted the latch, she found herself standing in a kitchen. She had barely taken in the room's massive proportions or the latest in kitchen design sitting cheek by steam oven with the original stone flags and heavy oak aged beams, when the niggle in her head solidified into a thought.

'How can this be a standing arrangement? You're meant to be on your honeymoon,' she blurted before she had considered the wisdom of reminding him where he might have been and with whom.

If the reminder had caused him pain, he was hiding it well. His inscrutable expression told her little, but that could be due to the fact that the dark shadow on his jaw and chin upped the dark, dangerous, moody stakes considerably.

'The plan had been for Elise to fly out to Maldives immediately. I intended to join her at the weekend.'

Her eyes went round. 'She was going on honeymoon *alone*?' Wasn't that taking independence a bit far?

'You have a comment to—' He broke off as two small dogs burst into the room, yapping loudly.

Mari watched as he bent to pat them, speaking to them in Spanish and showing more warmth for the animals than she'd yet seen him display to humans. Maybe he preferred them—she gave a half smile, as she did herself on occasion.

He straightened up just as a larger dog the size of a small donkey padded at a more leisurely pace into the room. The dog wagged its tail and stood placidly while he stroked its ears.

'You were saying…?'

Caught staring and with what she suspected might have been a soppy smile on her face, she glared. 'I wasn't, but, if you must know, if my new husband chose to spend the first few days of our honeymoon with his grandmother rather than me, I'd not be happy.'

'Well, he hasn't, has he?'

It took her a moment to catch his meaning. When she did she flushed. 'This isn't the same. It's business.'

'So you would expect your *real* husband to put you ahead of everything else—work, family, duty…? My grandmother will not be here forever.'

'Well, I'd have come with you obviously…I mean, hypothetically and not you…'

Their eyes connected and she saw a flicker of consciousness in his dark eyes before he bent to stroke one of the animals at his feet who, barometers of his mood, began to yap.

Who said animals and children knew? she

thought, watching as the larger dog began to lick Sebastian's hand with slavish devotion.

'What have you told your grandmother about me?'

Before Seb could respond a small bearded figure wearing a dressing gown and slippers shuffled into the kitchen. He carried a rifle, which he lowered when he saw Seb.

Deeply alarmed by the presence of a firearm, Mari had retreated instinctively behind the big scrubbed table. She relaxed slightly as the armed man wrung Seb's hand up and down and addressed him in excited-sounding Spanish.

Seb responded in the same language. He spoke for a few moments and then gestured towards Mari.

'Relax, it is not loaded.'

He said something to the older man, who looked Mari's way, laughed and put the rifle down on the table. He waved his hands, saying something to her slowly.

'Tomas says he is a harmless old man,' Seb translated, saying something that made the man laugh again. 'He says not to be afraid. I contacted him from the airport to say we would be arriving. My grandmother had already retired, but your room is ready.'

She managed a weak smile, which made the man tip his head in acknowledgement before he walked in the direction he had entered. Turning back, he gestured for her to follow him.

'Go. Tomas will show you to your room. If there's anything you want...'

Her eyes brushed his and she knew she was blushing. 'There won't be.'

CHAPTER EIGHT

THOUGH SHE WAS convinced she wouldn't be able to, Mari finally did drift off. She had no idea how long she actually slept, but it was still dark when she woke up, her body bathed in sweat, her heart thudding; only wisps of the nightmare remained. As they slipped away, reality came rushing in.

It was far worse than the creature that had been pursuing her in the nightmare.

'I'm married!'

It had been her secret dream, one she'd never even admitted to herself: her own home, a family and a man who she could drop her defences with, someone she could trust. She saw him in her dreams sometimes, but when she woke, his face vanished like smoke.

What have I done?

On the verge of panic, breathing hard, she sat bolt upright in bed, the crumpled sheets still clutched in her fingers.

She'd made a mistake, a terrible mistake! No, *mistake* wasn't a big enough word for what she'd done. *Eighteen months, Mari, that's all and then you can have your life back, and you'll never have to see him again.*

She flopped back and lay, one hand curved above her head, staring at the ceiling, seeing the shape of the dark exposed rafters against the white. Even though she had left the doors to the Juliet balcony open, the room was totally still, the only noise the soft swishing sound of the whirring fan. The silence pressed down on her like a weight. Her thoughts went round in circles like the fan as she tried to work out what was going to happen next.

She tried to block the negative thoughts. He liked dogs; he loved his grandmother... Oh, God, how had she got herself in this position?

She sat up again and her stomach rumbled. She knew from experience that a glass of warm milk was the only thing that would give her any more sleep that night. How far had it been to the kitchen?

She pushed back the covers, went across to her open case and took out the first thing she saw. It was a lacy shrug, and she pulled it on over the calf-length nightshirt she was wearing.

Outside her room the corridor, with its modern-art-treasure-sprinkled walls, was still lit at intervals by soft light from the wall sconces of beaten copper that had fascinated her when Tomas had led her this way.

Right, she was here, so what next? Right or left?

She remembered a wooden carving of a Madonna at the top of the flight of stairs, but there was no sign of that or, for that matter, the stairs, just lots of doors along both sides of the hallway, all heavy banded oak.

Right, Mari, it's hopeless. Go back to bed.

She ignored the good advice of the voice of common sense, unable to face the thought of lying there for the rest of the night. She was not ready to give up yet. She walked down to the end of the hallway that opened out onto what appeared to be a wrought iron Juliet balcony similar to the one in her bedroom, then with a sigh turned around.

She froze, the feral shriek of fear emerging from somewhere deep inside her… She opened her mouth and it just went on and on. The ghostly apparition screamed right back at her, and when she clamped her hand to her mouth, so did the spectral image that appeared to be floating in the distance.

Weak-kneed but smiling, she gave a shaky

laugh of sheer relief, and her reflection, framed in the massive mirror that filled the entire wall the opposite end of the corridor, laughed back at her.

Shaking with reaction, she grabbed the nearest thing for support; it was the big heavy metal handle of the door she stood beside.

'Ghosts don't have red hair.'

Even if he had been asleep the scream would have woken him; the visceral sound of terror made his blood run cold.

'*Mari...?*' Heart pounding, grim faced, he threw back the thin cover on the big carved oak bed that, had the room not been vast, would have dominated it and leaped out.

Seb hit the ground running, moving as if the devil himself were at his heels. Luckily the room was not in total darkness; a small lamp still burned on a desk in the corner of the room where the book he had abandoned earlier lay open. It illuminated the corner, casting a series of dappled shadows across the vaulted ceiling.

He grabbed the heavy oak door, pulling it hard enough to wrench the ancient wood off its hinges; it held even though it carried the extra weight of someone who was attached to the handle.

Unprepared for the violent lurch, Mari found

herself dragged without warning into the room behind the big door. She managed to keep her balance by holding the handle for dear life.

She barely registered the room itself. Her wide eyes developed a severe case of tunnel vision. Spectres were one thing, but flesh and blood and very real Seb clad in what seemed to be a pair of black boxers that hung low on his narrow hips and nothing else was another and far more disturbing proposition!

Her glance moved up in a slow sweeping arc from his bare feet. The farther she travelled, the hotter she got and the more squirmy the feeling in her stomach; her heart was beating harder than it had when she had faced the prospect of a ghostly haunting.

He was magnificent. He looked like some sculptured statue brought to life in glowing golden tones. There wasn't an ounce of surplus flesh on his body to blur the muscle definition of his ridged belly, shoulders and thighs.

Mari had no control over the series of breath-catching butterfly kicks in her stomach; she had never imagined a man could be so rampantly male. Before she had time or the ability to form anything approaching a rational thought, the cocktail of apprehension and excitement coalesced into a heavy ache low in her abdomen.

'I was looking for a glass of milk,' she heard herself say. 'I saw a ghost…' The protective screen of her lashes lifted. 'Not really but—'

'There are probably a few ghosts knocking around the place.' Holding her eyes, he pushed the half-open door closed with his foot.

Mari's glance went to the door and back to his face in a jerky, half-scared movement.

She was nervous. *He* was the one who should be feeling nervous, Seb thought… *Very* nervous. She was the one creeping around the place in the dead of night dressed like… Well, actually if she had not been dressed at all it could not have been any more provocative than the near transparent floaty number she had on.

The thing might be some modern take on Victorian primness, long-sleeved and fastened high at the throat with a little ribbon, but back-lit by the golden light from the lamp the white material became effectively transparent, the fabric so gossamer fine that if he tried, actually even if he tried not to, he could make out the dark perimeter of her rosy areola and the shadow between her thighs.

Mari ran her tongue across her lips to moisten them, struggling for some composure, and missing the resultant hot flare in his hooded glance.

She cleared her throat and turned her head,

saying conversationally, 'My, this is a big room.' *Big room—my God, could I sound any more inane?*

He had a cameo view of the classic purity of her profile, her hair a glorious fiery halo glowing under the subdued artificial light in the hallway, appearing dark against the pale and almost transparent whiteness of her provocative nightclothes.

She brought to mind one of the impossibly desirable virgin sacrifices in an old-fashioned horror movie that every dashing hero was determined to rescue and the villain wanted to lay.

As a fist of lust tightened in his groin Seb discovered his sympathies lay with the villain. He dragged a frustrated hand over his hair and reacted to the emotions spilling from her with a sardonic smile. This woman seemed to go from one emotional crisis to another. Did she not understand the meaning of restraint?

He understood it—he valued it because he had seen the sort of selfish excess and chaos that came with it—and yet understanding the meaning of restraint did not prevent his rampant hormones exploding. They overrode his iron control as his dark smouldering stare travelled slowly over her body.

'So what couldn't wait until the morning? Where's the fire?' He struggled to inject some amusement into his voice, but the combination of vulnerability and sheer unadulterated feminine sexiness had got to him in a place Seb had thought he'd hermetically sectioned, sealed off… when…

He couldn't remember exactly what age he'd begun to worry he'd inherited his parents' genes. It had kept him awake nights until he had realised that recognising your weaknesses meant they weren't going to trip you up; it was all about control.

Control, he told himself, struggling to recall the meaning of the word as he breathed his way through the conflicting needs to comfort her and tear off her clothes and sink into all that luscious softness.

'Fire?' she echoed, blinking up at him.

If there wasn't one, there would be—she looked hot enough to ignite anything within a fifty-yard radius, he decided, dragging his gaze from the plumpness of her trembling lips as he reminded himself that she might be as attractive as sin and twice as tempting, but Mari Jones was not destined to share his bed. Even if it hadn't been essential that he kept things on a professional footing, she was not the sort of woman he would have entertained having any sort of relationship with.

Even so, it would have been much simpler if

she had been unattractive or, for that matter, had one single flaw physically. His eyes moved from the fabric that had begun to cling with an electrostatic charge to the long shapely length of her legs, drawing his attention once more to the suggestion of shadow at their apex, and he forced himself to focus instead on the many flaws she had personality-wise.

The temper, he thought, sweating now, the mulish obstinacy, but most of all the sheer emotional excess in everything she did. She cried, she laughed, she screamed, she fought, and none of these things she did in moderation—he doubted she was even capable of it.

It didn't matter how pretty the packaging, he pitied the man who eventually tried to domesticate this red-headed witch. It would take a saint or someone equally capable of making a walk in the park a full-blown drama.

The thought triggered an image, a memory he'd thought he'd forgotten. The day his parents had managed to make such a harmless outing a front-page headline. The moment his mother had pushed his father into the lake had been caught on camera for posterity, as had been their making up, but what Seb remembered was the nauseous, churning sensation of shame in his stomach and the desire to vanish.

When he had run away from the scene, his

passionately reunited parents had not noticed their three-year-old son was missing until later that night.

The memory enabled him to claw back some semblance of control. He took a step back and stood there waiting.

Her stomach went into free fall as she glanced up at him through her lashes. He looked like the modern-day flesh-and-blood version of some sort of Greek god in his close-fitting boxers that did a very poor job of concealment, his dark hair standing up spikily, his jaw deeply scored with stubble. A primitive thrill shot through her body as she drank him in, in great greedy gulps.

'I'm sorry. It was a m-mistake.'

'Probably,' he agreed huskily. 'Calm down, you're shaking.' He caught her slim hands and pressed them between both of his.

The action might have been meant to soothe, but it did the opposite. Mari reacted to the contact like a cattle prod, throwing her arms wide to break the connection.

'I was looking for the kitchen. Do I go right or left?'

There was a long pulse of silence. It buzzed in her ears like a cloud of bees. Mari waited until it became unbearable.

'Did you hear what I said?'

He was so still, his stillness projecting a

tension that was evident in the skin taut over his face. The tension emphasised each slashing angle and perfect plane. Even at a moment like this Mari marvelled that a man could be that beautiful, not just aesthetically because of the sculpted outline of his lips or the symmetry of his bold features, but it was the underlying earthy quality that charged the air around him.

'This has been a long day. I'll get Tomas to fetch you—'

'Don't wake the poor old man, just tell me how to get there!' She struggled to flatten the panic she could hear in her voice. 'Please, Seb.'

She shook her head resolutely, too stressed to interpret the strange way he was looking at her, wishing he'd put on some clothes.

'You'll get lost. I'll show you,' he said, but didn't move.

'No!'

'Yes!'

They both spoke and moved at the same time, colliding.

Maybe he was a bastard; maybe he was just his parents' son. *You couldn't choose your genes, and why fight nature*? he thought as he reached for her. 'Later,' he murmured as he pulled her up hard against him and, one hand on her bottom, the other tangled in her hair, he pulled her head back and fitted his mouth to hers.

She melted into him, soft and warm, her arms going up to circle his neck as she gave a little sigh into his mouth, and kissed him back.

The hungry kiss went on and on, until with a groan he pushed her away and turned his back to her.

'Get out of here,' he growled. 'While you still can.'

The sudden rejection left her trembling. She could still feel the strength of his arms, the hardness of his erection against her belly. Mari bit her lip, and thought to hell with pride—she didn't care if he knew. She didn't care who knew. She wanted him, and if that meant begging she would, even at the risk of rejection!

'Let me stay, Seb, please. I don't want to go.' She had never wanted anything less in her entire life; she felt dizzy with the sweet hunger that coursed through her veins.

He swung back, took one look at her standing there and with a groan swept her up into his arms and stalked across to the bed with his prize.

He laid her on the bed and knelt beside her, sweeping her wild curls from her cheek and forehead, smoothing them out onto the pillow. The expression of fierce concentration on his face made her stomach flip.

One hand beside her face, he bent down and

kissed her softly, running his tongue along the inner surface of her lower lip, tracing the pouting outline before he slid inside, his tongue tasting every inch of the moist interior. His free hand moved to one breast, cupping it through the thin fabric, his thumb running up the lower slope to graze then tease the engorged rosy peak. Then he covered it with his mouth, wetting the fabric and drawing a hoarse cry of pleasure from her aching throat.

Mari arched up to him, tangling her fingers in his hair, feeling his big body curved over her, tensing a little as his hands slid under her nightshirt, up her thighs, then relaxing, her head pushing back into the pillow because it felt so good.

The sensations shooting through her felt like an electrical storm. The frantic feeling escalated until he suddenly levered himself upright.

Her blue eyes flew wide open in protest.

'You're overdressed.' At some point, Mari had no idea how or when, her little shrug had gone, but before she had time to consider how she felt about being naked in front of him he took the hem of her nightshirt in his two hands and pulled. The middle seam parted with a loud ripping sound until the only thing holding it together was the prissy little bow.

Holding her eyes with a wicked smile, he

very slowly undid the bow and peeled the fabric apart, then her insides dissolved some more as she closed her eyes and breathed in his scent. Warm and musky, it was intoxicating.

'Look at me.'

She did, her dark lashes parting to reveal the blue languid depths.

Lust slammed through him with a force that threatened to stop his heart, and what a way to go, he thought, drinking in the sight of her gorgeous wanton beauty. Her body was perfect, from the fullness of her high, firm breasts to her long, gorgeous legs that he was imagining wrapped around him.

'Have you any idea how much I want you?'

'I have some idea,' she said, daringly running her hand up his hair-roughened chest and belly.

He gave a low laugh and removed his boxers, drawing an ego-enhancing gasp from Mari.

The first skin-to-skin contact caused a flash of heat within her; the burning continued to build as he kissed her while touching her everywhere until she was on fire. She tensed as he parted her legs, then relaxed as the liquid heat flooded through her body, the pleasure bordering pain, it was so intense.

When he flipped onto his back and fed her hands onto his body she began to eagerly explore his warm, moist skin, fascinated by the overwhelming masculinity of his body, moving across the hard contours of his chest and down over the ridged muscles of his flat belly, while he lay, one hand hooked behind his head, watching her through gleaming hooded eyes.

It gave her a feeling of heady feminine power to curve her fingers around the hard, hot, silky column of his erection and hear him groan with pleasure. So much so that when he removed her hands and pinned them above her head she gave a cry of protest.

'I need to save some for you,' he whispered in her ear. 'Let me give you it all, Mari.'

'Please, oh, please!'

Her frantic plea ripped a lusty growl from his throat as he kissed her.

'I didn't sleep with Adrian.'

He lifted his head, and dark eyes glazed with passion blinked down at her. 'Good.'

'Or actually anyone.'

For a moment he lay above her perfectly still, every sinew strained, then she heard him mumble, low and sounding like someone in pain. 'Too late… Do you want me to stop?'

'No…no…' She trembled in anticipation, relaxing at the first shallow thrust, no explosion of pain just a feeling of intense pleasure… She let out a moan as he pushed deeper, his tongue sensually mimicking the more intimate movement of his hips.

Instinct made her wrap her legs around his waist as she arched under him, her body rippling tight around him, her fingers clawing at his back.

She clung to him as though he were the only thing stopping her vanishing into the sensual maelstrom that held her in its core as he was in her core, filling her with each stroke, pushing her higher and higher until— When it came, the fierce explosion drew a low keening cry from her throat. She grabbed hold of him and was saying his name over and over as she felt his hot release inside her, then he shuddered and rolled away.

For a moment she felt lost, then he pulled her to him, her head on his chest. She fell asleep listening to the heavy thud of his heartbeat.

He waited for the postcoital sense of *emptiness* that was the trigger for him to leave the warm bed. He never consciously acknowledged it, but if he had he would have considered it a perfectly reasonable price to pay for retaining control, keeping part of himself separate.

Instead Seb felt an utterly alien feeling of peace. Before he had a chance to ponder it another realisation hit: for the first time in his life, not only had he lost control, but he had not used protection. It had not been calculated, but some sixth sense told him that Mari was not going to give him the benefit of any doubt.

CHAPTER NINE

IN MARI'S DREAM someone was knocking on the door and calling...not her...not her name...and they were speaking a foreign language. It was fluid and nice to listen to but growing louder. Mari pushed free of layers of sleep and lay there smiling, feeling good, feeling... She stretched and muscles complained.

'Ouch!' She lifted a hand to smother a yawn and as the sheet, which was the only thing covering her, slid down she realised that she was naked... Naked, and where was she? The rush of recollection coincided with the door swinging inwards and then a woman's voice, the voice in her dreams, calling.

'Sebastian! Sebastian!'

Mari, now fully awake, responded to the emergency in the time-honoured fashion. She buried her head in the literal sense by sliding down to the bottom of the bed and heaving the covers that lay there in a tangled mess up over her unruly curls, tucking in her feet, her knees, her elbows…in an effort to disappear.

And that was it. Too late now to reconsider her actions—she was committed and also very uncomfortable.

In her concealment she held her breath, her heart thudding even faster at the thought of humiliating discovery. The muffled sound of heels on the floorboards got closer and the imperative tapping sound louder and louder. She held her breath in anticipation.

Totally convinced she was about to be discovered, Mari waited with the resignation of a condemned woman, wondering if it would be any less humiliating to reveal herself before her undoubted exposure. Should she test the theory and find out if a person really could die of humiliation, always supposing she didn't suffocate in the meantime?

Her oxygen-starved brain conjured up several versions of the headlines before she decided there probably wouldn't be any. Sebastian would hush it up to spare further embarrassment to the family name.

She was fast approaching the point where she had to breathe properly, even if that meant she was discovered. Just as her autonomic nervous system kicked in and she opened her mouth to

gulp in air, the sound was muffled by the creak
of a door opening.

'Mamina!'

She huddled down, knees drawn up to her
chest, trying to make herself as small as possible, into what she hoped would be mistaken for
a bundle of bedclothes by anyone who glanced
that way. So long as she didn't do anything
like... *Do not think about coughing, Mari,* she
told herself sternly.

It was hot. Sweat broke out over her skin,
making her situation even more miserably uncomfortable, and still they carried on talking...
Didn't he appreciate her predicament? Her teeth
clenched, she focused on breathing shallowly
while, the longer the conversation went on between Sebastian and the woman he had called
Mamina, the worse the skin-crawlingly awful
prospect of discovery became.

How humiliating would that be?

Just when she thought it couldn't get worse,
the muscles in her calf bunched, and she had to
bite down hard on her lip to stop herself crying
out. The torture of the cramp became so intense
that she was on the point of revealing herself
when the pain in her calf that extended all the
way to the arch of her foot began to diminish at
the same time she realised the flow of Spanish

had stopped and the tapping sound was moving towards the door.

A final word from the strong-sounding female voice and the door closed.

'You can come out now.'

The pile of bedclothes moved, the sardonic smile on Seb's face deepening into a broad grin as her head emerged, her hair gloriously tousled, her face deeply flushed a clashing shade of pink. She looked a long way from the sleeping angel with the cut-glass features and perfect profile he had reluctantly left to sleep, and even more touchable.

Indignation aside, Mari felt a lurch in her chest. If he smiled more often she'd be in serious trouble... What was she thinking? She was in serious trouble. She managed to keep her scowl in place as he levered his broad shoulders from the wall.

'My grandmother.' Keeping his eyes on her, he nodded towards the door.

'I figured *that* part out. What I couldn't work out was why you kept her talking for hours. You had to know that I was...'

He arched a sardonic brow. 'Hiding under the covers?'

When he put it like that...

'What was I meant to do?' she fired back. Struggling to retain a modicum of dignity, she held the sheet at shoulder height and eased herself up carefully into a sitting position, keeping her legs tucked underneath. She flexed her toes to ease the discomfort in the leg that had suffered the cramp attack.

'Well, let me see…how about introduce yourself?' he drawled.

'Oh, yes, that would have been fun! I'm your grandson's wife. I didn't know if she knew, or what story you'd told her!' she flung back.

Mari's bitter thoughts mingled with lustful ones as her wilful gaze roamed over him. He'd obviously stepped straight from the shower; presumably that was why he had not heard the knocking from the adjoining bathroom.

He had paused to pull on a towelling robe. His skin, still dusted here and there with moisture, looked vibrantly gold against the black fabric. Loosely belted around his middle, the robe ended midthigh, and Mari's glance lingered a fraction of a second too long on the hard, hairdusted columns of his heavily muscled thighs, triggering a tactile memory that pressed down on her as heavily and as hotly as his thighs had pressed her down into the mattress last night.

His dry voice cut into her carnal recollections. 'I thought you had a head-on approach towards most situations.'

Mari shook her head, the physical action helping to free her of the last clinging strands of the mind-numbing sensual fog. Adopting a cool expression, she lifted her chin and admitted, 'What seems a good idea at the time can seem a major mistake in the cold, clear light of day.'

An ice age could not have been more unexpected or as total as the frigid hauteur in his regard.

'So you have decided to draw a line under last night and call it a…mistake?' He sketched mocking inverted commas around the word as he bit it out through teeth bared in a hard, contemptuous smile.

Mistake? Wasn't that a pretty good analysis of the emotions that he'd been struggling not to analyse—his own 'head under the blanket' moment—as he'd stood accepting the sharp arrows of an icy-cold shower that had washed the scent of her off his flesh but not the memory of the sex, which seemed to have penetrated to a cellular level?

The light was not cold, but it was clear as it shone on her upturned features.

The fact that calling it a mistake was *exactly* what he'd been doing did not lessen the sense of outrage he recognised as totally irrational.

The confusion on Mari's face lifted. 'No… last night…' Did she regret it? 'I'm not talking about last night. I meant the wedding crashing.

Last night was…' Her voice trailed away. She couldn't say *special* to a man who had enjoyed God knew how many last nights… Just sex? For her it had felt like making love. She gulped past a ridiculous desire to weep. She should be glad that her first time had been so special. She knew a lot of people who hadn't been so lucky, and some of the stories had not made her regret her abstinence.

But then, she hadn't known what she was missing; now she did. Oh, God, what had she done? She had no answer, just a total aching certainty that if she had the opportunity to do it again she would.

'One would not have happened without the other.'

Unsure what to read into this statement, she nodded cautiously and eased one leg out from under her.

'And you'd still be a virgin.' Just saying it gave Seb the same gut-punch feeling he'd had last night.

Of course, he'd have been lying if he hadn't acknowledged that the fact he had been her first, that he had taken her to places no other man had, aroused him on a primal level. And though they were damped down, he could only assume that it was those fundamental male instincts that were now responsible for the uncharacteristic possessiveness he felt when he looked at her and the anger he had experienced when he had thought she could dismiss the previous night with a shrug of her elegant shoulders.

In order to hide the depth of her discomfort, Mari rolled her eyes and sighed. 'Oh, are we going to have *this* conversation?'

'I'm sorry if you find this boring, but yes, we are.'

She scanned his lean face and tilted her head in an attitude of astonishment. 'You're mad at me for being a virgin?' The discovery drew a laugh from her parted lips.

'I'm mad at you for not warning me sooner,' he rebutted grimly. He swallowed and dragged a hand over his wet hair, slicking it back from his bronzed forehead. 'I could have hurt you.' Passion was one thing, but to be as full on as he had been with someone totally uninitiated sent a heavy slug of fresh guilt through his body. It should have been gentle and tender...

Tender. Hell, it shouldn't have happened at all!

He looked at the top of her shiny head; it was all he could see. Her chin had dropped to her chest and her hair had fallen in a silky curtain across her face. It made him think of how it had felt. The ends had brushed his chest as she had slid down his body... He inhaled. No, he would not go there, and last night was a one-off. He had not been thinking with his brain, but that would change.

He was totally clear in his mind about this when her head lifted. She parted the hair that had fallen across her face with both hands and looked up at him through the fringe of her long lashes with eyes that shone like sapphires and whispered huskily, 'You didn't.'

As her soft full lips quivered into a slow smile that was both sexy and vulnerable, Seb felt his heart crash into his chest wall like a sledgehammer. Utterly unprepared, he had no protection from the powerful feeling.

'That's…' Without warning, a moaning gasp was wrenched from her lips. The sound pierced Seb like a dull blade as he surged forward in response to the cry of pain.

'What's wrong? What is it?' He sat on the side of the bed where Mari had her knee drawn up to her chest in an awkward tangle of limbs and sheet, and was clutching her calf.

Her lower lip was clamped between her teeth; she was as white as paper. 'Cramp!' she managed through clenched teeth.

'Is that all?' His relief was mingled with sympathy. He knew from experience how incapacitating a cramp could be, especially if you were a mile off shore when it hit; fate in the shape of an off-course kayaker had been on his side that day.

'*All?*' she choked. If she could have thrown something at him, she would have.

The pain that had earlier been limited to her calf now involved her foot, as well. Her toes had been pulled upwards by the strength of the muscle contractions and she had grabbed them in an attempt to ease the agony.

'Maybe I've got a pathetically low pain threshold but it hurts!' she wailed, ashamed of the weak tears that were leaking from her eyes.

'I know, believe me I do. Let me.'

'I can't.' She shook her head, refusing to release her grip on her foot.

'You can.' He calmly pulled her leg across his knees and began to work on the knots of muscle; the action of his long fingers immediately lowered the level of pain.

'Let go, Mari.'

He'd said that last night and it had worked out okay then; also his air of cool competence was reassuring. Still tensing at every fresh wave of pain, she fell back against the pillows, arms crossed on her forehead, eyes squeezed shut.

His hands on the smooth skin of her calf, he watched the sheet drawn across her chest rise and fall, thinking about what was underneath... He had apparently been taken over by a teenager.

Her eyes opened wide in protest, and she gave a little grunt of pain. 'Hey, that hurt!'

'Just relax.' It was advice he struggled to follow. What the hell had he been thinking of last night…and what was he meant to do today? Pretend it never happened? The memory of his reaction when he had thought that was what she was suggesting was still fresh in his mind.

Relax. *Easy for him to say,* she thought, closing her eyes again as he pressed harder on a knotted muscle, smoothing the kinks.

She complained again with a mumbled, 'Ouch!' But she kept her eyes shut. The compulsion to tense was lessening as his clever fingers worked up and down her calf and into the arch of her foot until her calf was relaxed and the spasms in her toes had stopped.

'That's good,' she breathed. A cupped hand above her eyes, the other now unfurled on the pillow above her head, she forced her eyelids apart and looked at him through glittering blue slits. 'You can stop now.'

He didn't, though. He carried on massaging her legs, his hands running up the silky soft insides in a slow advance-retreat pattern.

Feeling the sigh that rippled through her body, he raised her feet to his lips and pressed a soft kiss to the blue-veined arch of her narrow foot. Who knew that a foot could be sexy?

Who knew, she thought, feeling herself sink

into the mattress as delicious tingles zigzagged across her skin, that you had erogenous zones there?

'So how come you've never had a lover?'

She looked at him through her lashes. 'I have trust issues after a really terrible experience when I was being seduced. Actually, I was quite looking forward to it when this man appeared out of nowhere and called me a slut in front of the entire hotel.' She opened one eye to look at him in time to see a look of astonished comprehension flash across his face.

'I suppose he did me a favour, but I found it hard to think of it that way. It's bad enough discovering that the man you had spun romantic fantasy around was actually a sad serial seducer, but to have everyone there think I was some sort of slut who slept with married men…'

Seb closed his eyes and grimaced, seeing her face as it had been, no longer seeing the seductress mankind needed saving from but an innocent victim.

'He sounds a bit of a bastard,' he husked back throatily, as the things he had said came back in painful detail.

'Oh, they both were.'

'But six years, Mari…' he clenched out with a groan.

'Did I not say? I've a low sex drive.'

At her initial explanation his fingers had stilled. They moved again now, and the sound of his deep throaty laugh filled the silence, making the muscles low in her belly quiver.

'Oh, when you put it like that it's kind of obvious.'

She struggled to free her foot…but actually not so very hard, just a feeble kick, because his fingers were sliding higher now up the soft pale skin of her inner thigh, stroke then retreat, each time getting higher, but not high enough to satisfy the throbbing ache between her thighs. Her head turned on the pillow and she released a long, slow, sibilant sigh; the mixture of pleasure and frustration was exhausting.

'What the hell did you see in that creep?'

'I was eighteen, Seb. He singled me out from day one, encouraged me, took a real interest. A man had never done that before and I was flattered,' she admitted. 'And then one day I could see something was wrong. I waited after my tutorial and asked…' She lifted a hand to her head and groaned. 'I asked what I could do to help. It was then he admitted that he'd fallen for me. He'd been fighting it because he was my tutor and so much older. I was totally sucked in, and all the creeping around and secrecy seemed romantic.

'It turned out that everyone else but me knew

that at the start of an academic year he had an affair with a new student. It was a big standing joke—I was the joke.' The look she flashed him was rueful.

'You mean he groomed them.' At his sides Seb's hands clenched into fists. If the guy had been there at that moment he would have… He took a deep breath. He wasn't here but Mari was.

He'd taken a virgin bride. *What have you done, Seb?*

'We were all consenting adults, there was nothing illegal and I was pretty stupid.'

'He used his position of authority and trust,' Seb condemned. 'It is appalling that the college authorities allowed it to happen.'

'Well, I don't expect they knew,' she observed fairly. 'And they don't allow it, not now. There was a massive scandal the next year as the girl he singled out for special attention after me attempted suicide. Luckily she didn't succeed, but he resigned shortly after that and I think his wife divorced him. Don't stop…' she pleaded, lifting herself up on her elbows as he swore his contempt bilingually.

His eyes followed the flow of her hair as it settled over her shoulders, but he couldn't push back the hard knot of ice-cold anger that her matter-of-fact retelling of the story had created.

'I'm sorry about the things I said that night.

I had just come from a run-in with my mother, who was…well, being herself, and she never brings out the best in me.'

'It was a long time ago,' she said, looking at him curiously. 'And I had my revenge, so maybe we're even?'

'It left scars, and I was partly responsible for that.'

She held out her arms. 'You healed them, too, but there is this little one that I don't think you quite reached.'

A slow carnal smile curved his lips as he pulled her foot, tucking it over his shoulder. 'Now, where would that be?'

'Not sure,' she admitted thickly.

Seb found it, and he took his time about it; he had taken her to the edge twice before taking her over with him.

She flipped over on her stomach to look at him. 'I should go back to my room and get dressed.' She yawned without much enthusiasm. 'I don't know what your grandmother will think.'

'We are married, remember.'

A flicker of a frown disturbed her smooth brow as Mari looked at the ring on her finger, a plain gold band. 'But that's not real, is it? Though I suppose she won't know that.'

'My grandmother is no longer here. That

is why she—' his lips quirked at the corners '—stopped by, to say goodbye. She is staying with her sister for a few days. Apparently my great-aunt has had a fall.'

'Is she all right, your aunt?'

'Apparently she was more concerned about the horse.'

'Your aunt was riding?'

'In this instance, falling.' He threw back the quilt that had moments before warmed both their bodies and casually vaulted from the bed, completely at ease with his naked state. Mari was less so, but her glance welded hungrily on his long, lean, muscle-toned frame, and she felt her insides heat.

Their glances connected and she lowered her gaze, clearing her throat. The microsecond of contact sent her nervous system into chaos… *My God, I've become insatiable.*

'You don't sound very worried,' she observed, visualising a scene in her head that involved him crossing the room and slipping back into bed…into her. 'Should she even be on a horse at her age?'

The reproach in her tone drew a laugh, and a look over his shoulder as he moved in the opposite direction to her imagination to the window, which he pushed wider, letting in the smell of jasmine with a soft breeze.

'Marguerite fully intends to die on one, as she will tell anyone who dares suggest she should slow down, but not yet, I think, though reading between the lines it sounds as though she was shaken.'

She glimpsed the concern behind the languid humour and touched the smooth skin of his back as he sat down on the bed to slide his jeans on before standing to zip them up.

'Why don't you hate me, Mari?'

She blinked, astonished by the question. 'Who says I don't?'

She glimpsed a strange look on his face before he turned and stalked across the room, making her think of a panther. 'Because you don't have it in you.' Although what he had to say might severely test that theory.

'I did crash your wedding and nearly cost you a billion dollars.'

'I tricked you into marrying me.'

'There have been some upsides to that,' she admitted, looking from his face to the tumbled bedclothes. At least in bed naked she had no trouble understanding him. 'And I'm not eighteen anymore. I knew what I was doing. I admit I never expected to enjoy anything about these eighteen months.'

Even from the several yards that separated them she could see the lines of strain around his mouth as he began to walk back across the room towards her, looking very like her mental image of a dark, dangerous pirate with his bare feet, rippling muscle, his chest gleaming gold and the stubble on his face giving him a dangerously attractive look of dissipation. In a fair world it would be illegal for a man to be this sexy.

So the world is not fair, Mari—deal and stop drooling! She was dragging her eyes clear of the open fastener on his waistband when he spoke, his deep voice just audible above the blood rushing in her ears.

'Has it occurred to you that the eighteen-month rule might be out of the window?'

Utterly confused, Mari searched his face, looking for a trace of the warm, sensitively passionate lover who had taught her so much about her own body in just one night, and morning… but he wasn't there. Just a sombre-faced stranger, not the man she had fallen… The blood drained from her face as she swallowed and thought, *No, I can't have… It's just sex. Very good sex, but just sex. Love is—*

'Unless you are on the pill?'

Too busy arguing with herself, she still didn't see where he was going with this. 'Why would I be?'

'I didn't use anything. You could be pregnant.' Her comment about not wanting children had not seemed relevant at the time; now it did.

His words hit her with the force of a lightning bolt. She gasped and hit back, fear making her voice cold. 'Do you make a habit of having un-protected sex with one-night stands?'

His dark eyes glittering, the sharply defined contours of his high cheekbones were accentu-ated by a dull flush as he ground out what she was assuming—no major leap—was a swear word and dragged a hand across his set jaw.

'It was a first. I'm sorry.'

She gave a sniff, feeling guilty now that she had lashed out at him. At the end of the day, she'd become just as caught up in the moment and had behaved just as recklessly as Seb had. 'So am I. It's as much my fault as yours,' she acknowledged.

Seb gave a hard laugh. 'I seriously doubt that many people would agree with you, and you are not a one-night stand. You are my wife.'

'For eighteen months…'

'Maybe.'

'What do you mean?' she demanded, gather-ing the quilt around her.

'I mean if last night results in a baby, that time limit vanishes. There is no way that my child would be brought up by another man.'

When she finally spoke, her voice sounded

weirdly controlled, perhaps to compensate for the total chaos rampaging in her head. 'I'm not having a baby.' *And I'm not in love.*

'You're right. It probably won't happen. Why don't we deal with it when or if the time arises?'

She shook her head. 'You really are unbeliev-able. How am I meant to think about anything else now? It would be a disaster!' she wailed, thinking *disaster* was not a big enough word to describe being trapped in marriage with a man who didn't love you. She had always felt sorry for those people who 'stayed together because of the baby' and she didn't want to be one of them!

His jaw tightened. 'What are the odds?'

Confused by the abrupt question, she shook her head.

'Of you conceiving.'

'Oh.' She flushed self-consciously and did a quick mental calculation and swallowed. 'Pretty high,' she admitted. 'Why is this happening?' She pressed her face with her hands and released a muffled wail. 'I can't have a baby!'

'Calm down.' He sat down on the bed and brought her hands together, covering them with his. 'I know you don't want children but—'

'Who said I didn't want children?' she flared.

'You did.'

'Not my own—there are so many children out there who need homes. I'm going to adopt.'

He pressed his fingers to the bridge of his nose and closed his eyes, wondering if he could feel any more of a total bastard.

'What? What have I said now?'

He shook his head.

'So what now? You're the one who said he was good at thinking on his feet.'

The slow dangerous smile that split his lean face did not lessen the tension that drew the skin taut across his high cheekbones. 'I am thinking, but you are distracting me.'

She followed the direction of his gaze and pulled the quilt up over her breasts, before angling a hot-cheeked look of accusation at his face. 'You're thinking about sex at a time like this?'

'I can multitask,' he promised her. 'How does this work for you? We cut the honeymoon a bit short and go straight back to Mandeville, at least until we know for sure one way or the other. We'll need to consult with an obstetrician. There are probably a few things you should and shouldn't be doing.'

'Stop it. I am not some sort of...incubator!' A short while ago she had been a desirable woman he had wanted to make love to; now she was what...a mother?

A mother... A shiver of reaction worked its

way through Mari's body as the words echoed in her head.

At least now she knew the answer to *one* of the questions she had been asking herself on and off virtually all her life. While she still didn't know what made any mother abandon her child, she did know that she never could.

Facing the slim possibility there might be a baby, Mari knew that nothing in the world would make her give it up. She knew, but what about Seb? Would he ask her to? Would he assume she'd have a termination?

'Don't be ridiculous! Look, I didn't plan on having a family now either, but—'

She wanted to cry, but instead she tuned him out. It was ironic really; she had guarded her heart so well all those years, and the first time she let down her guard... God, she had terrible taste in men. At least she hadn't fallen for him.

You keep on telling yourself that, Mari.

'What happens if I am pregnant? What, as a matter of interest, is your grand plan? I'm sure you've got one.'

'Isn't it obvious?'

She tensed. 'Not to me.'

'We stay married.' He angled a searching look at her face. 'You look surprised. What did you think I was going to say?'

She shook her head. 'What about love?'

'We are not talking song titles here, Mari. We are talking about giving our child, should there be one, a secure upbringing.'

'There might not be a child,' she reminded him. The addition was for her own benefit. 'Probably won't be.'

He nodded and looked at her. 'But until we know for sure…Mandeville?'

Reluctantly she nodded.

CHAPTER TEN

THE MOMENT THE private jet landed, Mari's phone began to ping. She fished it out and saw there were a dozen missed calls and twice that many texts, all from her brother.

She scrolled through a couple and found they were all much the same.

Where the hell are you? Come and rescue me, I think I'm dying, the doctors are quacks.

Her finger was poised above Dial when she paused.

Seb was a lying monster, but the law of averages dictated that even lying monsters were right sometimes. He had predicted that Mark would react this way, and she was conditioned to respond as she always did.

Was it time to break the cycle, not just for her but for Mark?

Very slowly she closed the phone and dropped

it back into her bag. She knew that Seb was watching her but she refused to give him the satisfaction of knowing that she had followed his advice.

They had hardly said a word since they left Spain. Once or twice Seb had tried to initiate a conversation, but she had cut him off.

On the way across to the waiting limo she stopped and looked up at him. Despite everything her insides quivered. He looked so incredible.

'I'm sorry I've been sulking.' Actually she had been punishing him for not being in love with her, which, when you thought about it, was pretty pointless. She should be grateful he wasn't pretending.

Seb tilted back his head and dug his hands into the pockets of his well-cut trousers, a smile chasing like a shadow across his sombre features.

'Had you? I hadn't noticed. I'm probably overreacting,' he admitted in return, 'but if we'd stayed in Spain my grandmother would have given us no privacy.' Which had been part of the reason he had chosen to take her there.

The idea that his grandmother's presence would have made it easier to keep her at arm's length, keep his hands off her, seemed frankly laughable now. He could see now that he'd been in denial about the strength of his attraction to her. Logically, taking her to his bed should have diminished that hunger, but if anything it had grown during the short time they had been together.

'*If* there is a child and that remains a massive if, there will be things we need to discuss without ears at doors. You'll like Mandeville. It's a great place for a child to grow up—there's plenty of room.'

The words came back to Mari as she got her first glimpse of the white Palladian mansion with its rows and rows of perfectly symmetrical windows. She snatched an awed breath. Plenty of room? It was the size of a city!

'Ever so humble, but home.'

He covered her hand with his; for a moment he thought she was going to leave it there, and then she didn't. His jaw clenched; the rejection, a small thing, had a sting that was out of proportion to its size.

Mari didn't look at him, just stared straight ahead as she nursed her hand in her lap. 'This place is pretty daunting, the idea of servants and—'

'You'll be fine. I actually think you could cope with anything, and it is big, but that could work well. You can still have your privacy.'

'So you won't be here? No work, obviously...

but when you say *space*, does that mean we won't be sharing a room?' She closed her eyes and thought, *Did I say that out loud*?

'Mari Jones, the first time I saw you I wanted you.'

Mari opened her eyes.

'And I still do,' said the man who was famed for playing it cool. 'We will be sharing a bed.'

He saw a flicker in her eyes and wondered if she wanted to hear something else. He took her hand and felt the zing of electricity shoot up his arm.

'The sex was sensational.' He wasn't in *love*, he was in *lust*. He didn't *need* her, he *wanted* her, and that made all the difference.

It was odd, Mari reflected—she hadn't even known until that precise moment how much *more* she wanted. Much more than what he was offering or would ever offer. It was not until she heard him carefully avoid the word and felt the pain of its absence that she stopped trying to pretend that she had fallen in love with him.

God, could life be more complicated?

Normally Seb could read her expressions, but he struggled to read the look she gave him, and was further thrown by the odd intonation in her soft voice when she spoke.

'How about we just enjoy ourselves?' she suggested easily.

He frowned. That was his line, and he felt irrationally irritated to hear her speak that way.

'Until we know for sure.'

He nodded and struggled to stifle a restless sense of dissatisfaction.

When she had first walked into the place Mari had been utterly convinced that she would never feel at ease in the dauntingly grand surroundings. The ballroom at Mandeville was straight out of a fairy tale, and the walls held the sort of art collection that a major gallery would envy, not to mention the massive leisure suite with a full-size swimming pool tucked away in the lower ground floor, but three weeks in Mari had adapted to the space and elegance with amazing ease.

It might be *unadapting* she had the problem with, she realised uneasily.

It was hard not to compare the life of a child growing up here with one growing up in her tiny fourth-floor flat—not that it was about money. Mari knew, none better, that it was love and security that really counted.

But Seb would make a good father. It wasn't just his genuine desire to *be* a parent; he had a lot to offer. Seeing him interact with his young half-sister, who obviously adored and respected him, made her realise how far out in her initial assessment of him she'd been.

And being around him so much Mari found herself falling deeper and deeper in love with him every day. Sometimes the sheer hopelessness of it all made her seek a quiet corner and weep, although that might be the hormones.

She knew that she was pregnant. She had known for a week now. The little changes—she had no morning nausea, thank God, but she'd gone off coffee completely, and her breasts were painfully sensitive.

She had not confided in Seb, who didn't even trust a home testing kit. He insisted they have the test done by a Harley Street specialist, totally unnecessary, but she knew better than to try to dissuade him.

He'd been right. It had worked…worked *too* well really, she mused. It was all so *polite*. They hadn't had a single disagreement; there was no sparking off each other; it was all totally *vanilla*, which on the surface sounded good but in reality felt flat and unreal… Yes, that was the right word, *unreal*. There were times when she felt they were actors in a play, performing to an unseen script. She could only assume that was what he thought a good relationship should be.

The only time it felt normal was in bed. That was when the stilted politeness went out of the window, and it got raw and real… It was those nights that kept her going!

She was living for sex—that didn't sound healthy, but it was fun—while it lasted. And that was the point: how long would it last? Then they would be polite or maybe resentful strangers, the only thing holding them together a child.

When the consultant walked back into the office, Seb, who had sat in a chair opposite her trying to channel relaxed, surged to his feet.

'Congratulations.'

He had his back to her, so Mari couldn't see his expression, just the tension in his broad shoulders. It was gone when Seb exchanged a manly handshake with the other man and put a hand under Mari's elbow as she rose, as though she were already burdened by a pregnancy bump.

On the drive back he was unnaturally silent. It wasn't until they turned into the parkland that he slowed the car and stopped.

'Are you all right with this?'

She didn't respond.

'Aren't you excited?' With a frown he searched her face. 'Happy…sad…angry…?'

Crazily, she welcomed the shade of irritation that had crept into his voice.

'I already knew,' she admitted.

He stared at her for a moment before blasting, 'Then why the hell didn't you tell me?'

'Because you wouldn't have believed me!' she flung back, feeling her energy levels rise as she fed off the static charge in the air that had been so absent in the past weeks.

His head went down, concealing his face, but she could see his shoulders lifting as he took several long deep breaths. When he lifted his chin from his chest his expression was *pleasant*... Now, there was a word she had never imagined she'd think in the same sentence as Seb Rey-Defoe.

'You're right...' A muscle clenched in his lean cheek before he added, 'I'm sorry.'

She sucked in a furious breath, the anticlimax sending her spirits into a downward spiral. 'It was probably my fault.'

Hating the dispirited note in her voice, he bit back a retort. He really didn't know how long he could keep this up.

The harder he tried, the more distant she seemed to become. He had turned himself inside out trying to show her that living together did not have to be a constant battle. Did she appreciate how hard he was trying?

He'd have believed that she was indifferent to him if it weren't for the fact that she was so insatiable in bed, and utterly uninhibited. He lived for those nights!

'So I was thinking we're officially married now as opposed to being temporarily married.'

As opposed to what we'd have been if I weren't pregnant, she thought, looking out of the window to hide the hurt.

'There's a dinner at the end of the week, if you feel up to it—the royals are guests of honour.'

'I'm not ill, I'm pregnant.'

'Of course,' he said, reminding himself that he needed to show he could be sensitive to hormones…sensitive, but not mention them—not as easy as it sounded. 'I thought you'd like to officially be my hostess.'

'Fine.'

That word had come back to haunt her on several occasions since.

The brisk walk through the park was not as relaxing as she'd intended. It was hard to forget tonight and relax when you couldn't escape the reminder in the form of the magnificent facade of the house. It wasn't just geography—the gardens had been designed with the vast Palladian mansion as the focal point. Like disapproving eyes, the rows of windows seemed to follow her.

She brushed away the fanciful notion, laughing at her overactive imagination and frowning at her nerves. Under the calm exterior—actually she was no longer so sure her calm, approaching comatose attitude had fooled anyone—Mari was eaten up by nerves. She felt so out of her depth that she was a stumble away from gibbering terror.

'Don't be a wimp.' Above her stern voice the clock in the bell tower pealed out the half hour. With a deep sigh Mari squared her shoulders. She had timed it like a military operation so that she wouldn't be dressed too soon and waiting in the wings twiddling her thumbs while she watched the second hand tick. She quickened her pace—she didn't want getting ready to be a mad dash either.

The massive front door was flung open to allow access for the army of people who were preparing for this 'simple little dinner party'. Everyone had a task, and no one seemed to notice Mari as she walked through the marble-floored hallway filled with light streaming in from the cupola overhead.

The double doors to the formal dining room were still open. As she slowed then paused to watch the hive of activity, she felt more than a little like a child who'd sneaked downstairs to watch from a distance the grown-ups' party.

The long dining table was as much of a work of art itself as the massive chandelier that lit it.

The place settings all arranged with geometric precision, the napkins all perfectly aligned, the glasses gleaming, it groaned with the weight of silver and crystal.

As she stepped into the room, one of the team of florists that had spent the afternoon filling the house with more than the normal quota of massive formal flower arrangements saw Mari and smiled a little nervously.

'Is there a problem, Mrs Rey-Defoe?'

The woman, a girl who was probably her own age, was waiting for her approval. The idea was somehow more shocking than the prospect of hosting a dinner party where the glittering guest list included several diplomats, a Hollywood A-lister, the witty writer of a political column and a scarily famous athlete.

Mari smiled. 'Everything looks marvellous. I wish I had your talent. All I can do is throw some flowers in a vase and hope for the best.'

'Oh, the natural look is very in at the moment.'

They both laughed, and as the conversation progressed it turned out that the girl had been brought up in a village near to where Mari's foster parents lived. They chatted a while before Mari, conscious of the time, made her way reluctantly towards the curving staircase.

Her hand was on the smooth curving banister

when she felt the change in the air and the familiar prickle on the back of her neck. She turned her head and knew he'd be standing there. Seb, already dressed for dinner and looking incredible enough to make her sensitive stomach do a double backflip. He was standing framed in the doorway of one of the many rooms that fed directly off the hallway. Through the open door she could see the book-lined walls of the library, which he used as a study.

Her fingers tightened, knuckles white on the banister. If theirs had been a normal relationship, she would have gone over and straightened his tie, which was of course already straight—everything about Seb was always immaculate, a fact that should not have made her throat ache but it did.

Hormones. The word, she reflected, had become a bit of a mantra. Every time she had a confused thought or feeling she fell back on the excuse. She was saying it a lot at the moment.

Seb watched the animation he had seen in her face as she'd laughed and chatted with the florist fade, replaced with a wariness that she seemed to reserve specially for him.

'I was just going to get ready,' she said defensively.

He shrugged, not concerned that she would keep him waiting, or that she would look anything less than incredible. Most of the women he knew would have spent half the day getting ready for a formal event, but he'd seen Mari step out of the shower, pull on the first thing that came to hand, run her fingers through her hair, gloss her lips with something clear and shiny that tasted of strawberries and look breathtaking.

'It was just the florist lived near the village where my foster parents…'

He dragged his eyes from the temptation of her strawberry lips and cut across her rambling defence with a flash of anger. 'You think I have a problem with you talking to someone who arranges flowers? Do you really think I'm such a snob?'

'Not a snob, no,' she admitted.

He treated everyone the same, which didn't mean he hung out with the staff; apart from a handful of close friends, he appeared to keep everyone at a distance regardless of their social standing. And he didn't seem to notice how hard people worked to please him, and they did. She'd seen it time and time again—they went the extra mile to get his approval.

Had she become one of them?

'So you'd be fine with me seeing Annie so-cially… The gardener or the cook or the—?' She paused and dragged in a deep sustaining breath thinking, *Calm, Mari, calm*.

'I think they would be uncomfortable with the situation. Whether you like it or not, your position—'

Anger, sudden and hot, spurted up. He didn't have a clue! 'What position?' she blurted, and saw shock in his face but she couldn't stop herself. Weeks of saying the right thing had made her feel like a ticking bomb.

'I've been stuck in this place all week.' Her hand lifted in a graceful gesture encompassing the stately elegance around them. 'The only time I see you is in bed. I miss my work…the children. I'm lonely. I'm bored…' She clamped her lips over the quiver of embarrassing self-pity and steeled herself for his response, fully expecting him to point out that there were no bars on the windows, there was no bolt on the doors.

In her head she could hear him saying, *If it's so bad, what's keeping you here*?

Would she be brave enough to answer him honestly, admit that she stayed for him?

To be near him.

To hear his voice.

Would she ever be brave enough to admit that she loved him?

Well, she didn't find out, because once again she had made the mistake of thinking she could anticipate his reaction.

Lonely—the catch in her voice, all his internal debate, all his endless mental pro and con lists suddenly meant nothing, because he could see himself losing her. As he imagined her walking out of the door, out of his life, the knot in his stomach was fear. He called himself all the insults in his vocabulary, which was extensive, and still they didn't begin to describe what an utter fool he'd been.

His first mistake had been thinking he could take emotions out of marriage; on paper it had equalled no tensions. He had wanted his life to resemble the clear, uncluttered lines of his desk—neat rows, square edges, controlled, no mess—and it could. It *had* been, but as he looked into Mari's stormy, beautiful face, he made a life-changing discovery—he no longer wanted it to.

Love— He had avoided even thinking the word. Love was what had changed everything, had changed him.

He didn't want a suitable bride, someone who said the right things and agreed with everything he said. He wanted Mari. Not the Mari that said what she thought he wanted to hear, but the one who blurted out the first thing that came into her head and argued the hind leg off a donkey just for the hell of it—he wanted *his* Mari back!

'You are totally wrong.'

Hanging on the banister, she took two steps up then, unable to stop herself, one down, but she didn't lower her wary guard as she struggled to read beyond the cool detachment of his manner, to read the expression in his deep-set eyes.

'I am?'

'About me and us… Your position is…' He stopped, his dark brows twitching into a straight line as he framed his suspicious question. 'Has anyone here treated you with less than respect?'

The negative shake of her head lessened the explosive quality of his hard stare; the nerve in the hollow of his clenched cheek stopped jumping.

'We should stay married.'

'I know, because of the baby,' she said dully.

'Because you are you and I am…' He sucked in a deep breath, then let it out slowly before saying in a voice that vibrated with emotion, 'Lonely.'

Mari watched in disbelief as, having dropped the unexploded conversational bomb at her feet, he turned to go back into the study, pausing to call casually over his shoulder, 'Join me here for a drink when you're ready—tonic, lime and lots of ice?'

The door closed.

CHAPTER ELEVEN

WHEN THE FEELING returned to her paralysed limbs, Mari flew on an adrenaline rush high up the stairs two at a time, her heart thumping against her rib cage.

By the time she reached the bedroom where her clothes were laid out, ready, she had come back down to earth. He had waited to say this until *after* he knew about the baby—was that significant?

And after all, what had he said— *Lonely...?* It might just mean he was at a loose end.

Was she seeing and hearing what she wanted to?

Fingers pressed to her temple, she closed her eyes and willed the inner dialogue to stop before her head exploded, which was not a good look for the perfect hostess.

Her eyes shot wide as she pushed up the cuff of her sweater to see the time.

'Oh, God!'

She stripped off her clothes as she walked across the room. She entered the bathroom, where she proceeded to chuck half a bottle of some expensive bath oil in the bathtub and turned on the taps full. While the tub filled she piled her hair on top of her head, skewering in the pins carelessly before lowering herself into the water.

By the time she had stepped into the black number that managed to be both classy and extremely sexy, Mari had managed to achieve a degree of composure, even if it was skin-deep. Underneath she was so wound up she wasn't sure if she'd be able to wait for him to explain what the hell he had meant. She had a horrible feeling that the moment she saw him she was going to blurt out something terminally stupid like 'I love you!'

Well, he'd either run, laugh in her face or… anything was better than this terrible uncertainty.

Seb took the box out of his pocket. It should have been a ring, he thought, snapping it open to glance down at the string of sapphires that had caught his eye as he passed a shop. He could see them around her lovely neck, the colour a tribute to her eyes. He slid the box back into his pocket and pushed his head into the big wing-back chair that faced the fireplace.

Some inner sixth sense made him glance up just as a figure appeared outside the open French doors. The overalls the man was wearing were emblazoned with the name of the catering company who had been brought in to bolster his own kitchen staff.

The obvious assumption would be that he had lost his way, but his furtive manner told another story. As Seb made these observations, the man looked over his shoulder to check there was no one to see him before he stepped inside the room.

'Very nice,' he said softly as he looked around the book-lined room.

Interesting, Seb decided—the mirror was angled in a way that made it possible for him to watch the man without the intruder being aware of his presence in the room.

The figure in the overalls was moving with increasing confidence now; he even began to whistle a slightly off-key tune through his teeth as he walked around the room picking up objects, turning them over like an expert before replacing them or, in one or two instances— the man definitely had an eye or, as his grandmother would have put it, he knew the cost of everything and the value of nothing—putting them in his pocket.

He spotted the cupboard containing Seb's grandfather's collection of Georgian silver, smiling broadly as he did so, and Seb had his first full-face look at the guy.

A shaft of startled recognition turned Seb's curiosity into something far more personal—something cold, very cold. Ironically at one point the man had picked up the file that told Seb all he needed to know about his intruder and a lot he didn't want to know about George Laxton…Francis…Richie…Griffiths, a small sample of the aliases that this moderately successful conman went by.

The contempt etched on Seb's face gave way to alarm; his eyes went to the door that Mari could walk through at any moment.

That was one introduction he didn't want to make.

If ever he felt a twang of conscience about his decision to keep her in the dark, he reminded himself that if Mari had wanted to know her parentage she would have put the wheels in motion herself, so what she didn't know… *It would hurt her.*

When he'd decided originally to look into her parentage he had debated the ethics of it, but had gone ahead despite his misgivings, tempted ultimately by the idea of producing the loving mother he knew Mari secretly longed for.

When he'd got the information back it had turned out to be no fairy-tale ending: her mother had died from an accidental overdose after she had abandoned her children.

But Amanda was a victim, too, in a way. Her married lover, Mari's father, had served time for bigamy, and was the true villain of the story. So what was that villain doing here in his home?

It was a question for another time. Right now, the priority was to make sure that his and Mari's paths did not cross.

He was halfway to his feet, unnoticed by the figure, who was now efficiently emptying the contents of the silver cabinet into his capacious pockets, when the door did open.

Pausing, Seb sank back down into his concealment. It was hard to watch and wait, but if he wanted this man out of Mari's life forever it would be useful to have a bargaining chip. A pocket full of valuables and the threat of a prison term could be that lever.

Mari paused outside the door. Should she knock? No, she decided, boldly pushing it open, that would be too 'schoolgirl at the headmaster's office'.

'Oh!'

It was a massive anticlimax—the library was not empty, as a middle-aged man, one of the caterers, was there, but of Seb there was no sign.

The last thing she wanted to do was hang around, as she wanted to find Seb, but politeness made her linger. As she did the oddness of this man's presence struck her. Why was he here, in the room that was Seb's private sanctum?

The man, who was staring at her a little too intently for comfort, showed no sign of filling in the blanks without a push.

'Hello, can I help you…?' She stopped, her smooth brow furrowing as she scanned the stranger's face. She was pretty sure she had never met him but…

'Have we met already? You look a little familiar…' The likeness almost in her grasp, it slipped away.

The man grinned, and for no reason at all a frisson of unease slid down Mari's spine. Struggling against a growing antipathy, she smiled weakly back, but also took a cautious step back towards the door.

'Now, that is nice—early Georgian. A real collector's item.'

To Mari's utter amazement, without even trying to hide what he was doing, the man slipped the miniature he had held out to admire into a pocket in his overalls, one that she noticed was already bulging…with other stolen items? The bold thief was either mad or… Actually he was obviously mad, but not, she hoped, violent.

'That's stealing. Put it back immediately and we'll forget all about it!'

'Stealing…?' The man rubbed his hand along the goatee he sported. 'Now, me, I like to call it a redistribution of wealth.' He bared his yellowy teeth in a cold smile. 'I'd know you anywhere, darling—you're the living spit of your mum.'

Mari, who had moved towards the door to call for help, froze; the colour drained from her face as she spun back. She could hear the pounding of her heart in her ears. It sounded like the waves crashing on a distant seashore. 'You know my m…mother?'

'Knew. Amanda is no longer with us, sadly.'

'She's dead.' Her thoughts whirled, an unrelenting flow of question marks running through her head.

Was he telling the truth? What reason did he have to lie? 'My mother was called Amanda?'

'You're a lot bigger than her. She was a tiny little thing, except of course when she was carrying you and your brother.'

For a few moments she'd had a mother. It was crazy to feel bereft, but Mari did. A solitary tear slid down her cheek. While she hadn't known, there was always the hope that one day their mother would come looking for them… She would explain why she'd had to abandon the babies she loved. It had been a childish game she had played, one she should have put away with her dolls, and yet she had clung to the comfort the possibility offered, even though she knew deep down that it was never going to happen.

Now she knew for sure it was never going to happen.

'Don't look so sad, sweetheart.'

'Who are you?'

White-knuckled hands gripping the leather armrests, Seb closed his eyes. Keeping his anger in check was taking every ounce of his energy. He knew what was coming and he couldn't stop it. He had to let it run its course and then be there for her. He ached for her pain—as if she hadn't had enough pain in her young life.

'I'm hurt you don't recognise your old dad.'

Mari's eyes, very blue in her paper-white face, widened. She stood still as a statue, and she shook her head in a slow negative motion of denial; he couldn't be her father.

'I think you'd better leave now,' she said firmly. 'Before I call Security. Just put the miniature down and walk away.'

'My, quite the little princess, aren't we? But you've done well for yourself,' he conceded. 'It has to be said you've really fallen on your feet.'

He looked around the room and gave an approving nod.

'If you don't leave now, I'm afraid I'll have to report you to your employer.'

He gave a hoot of laughter; the sound was not pleasant. 'I'm not on the payroll, but this—' he touched the logo emblazoned on his chest with a touch of smug pride in his voice '—made it a lot easier to get in here.'

'You're not my father.' *Say it often enough and you'll believe it, Mari.* Silencing the voice of her subconscious but not the quiver of uncertainty in her voice, she lifted her chin. 'I don't have a father.'

'Look again, my lovely.' He pointed to his face, watching hers, his narrow eyes no longer smiling.

Startled as much by his change of accent as the invitation, she allowed her eyes to rest on the face of the man who claimed to be her father, which was ridiculous. He was nothing like any of the visions she had of her parent. She and Mark had always…Mark. Pressing a hand to her stomach in an effort to counter the sick churning inside, she understood why his face had seemed so familiar. It was no individual feature, nothing was identical, similarities were blurred, but it was there in the slant of the eyes and the curve of the lips, though her brother's was fuller and inclined to petulance and not meanness.

She lowered her lashes in a protective shield, but not, it seemed, before the man—she couldn't even think of him as a father—read her expression.

He gave a crow of triumph.

Pride came to her rescue. She lifted her chin and looked at him levelly. 'Why are you here?'

'To see my daughter.'

'After twenty-four years?' She eyed him warily, struggling not to show the fear that was building inside her, focusing instead on her anger. 'You know *nothing* about being a father, a parent,' she flashed, smiling as she realised that her child would have a father, the sort of father who would give his life for his child.

'Don't worry. I don't want to hang around any more than you want me here,' he snarled, visibly unsettled by the change in her manner. 'It's just I'm a bit short of cash at the moment and you're… We could call it a loan.'

Mari felt physically sick. This man was her father… She gave a shudder of revulsion and wondered when this nightmare would stop. 'I don't have any money.'

'But your husband does—pots of the stuff.' He rubbed his hands together in gleeful anticipation of the luck that had come his way.

'How did you find me?'

'Saw your picture in the paper, knew you the moment I saw who you were—amazing. You were an ugly little thing when you were born, red and screaming.' He gave a shudder of distaste.

'I have no money,' she repeated flatly.

'But you can get it. I don't think your posh husband is going to be quite so keen if he finds out your dad has a prison record. Can't you see the headlines now?'

This overt attempt at blackmail took her breath away. She looked at him in utter disgust. It was not often that you came across someone without a single redeeming feature, but it seemed that her biological father was one of those people. It was hard to face, but it was the cold, stark truth, and better to face it and move on.

A great sentiment, but at that moment all she wanted to do was weep until she had no tears left.

'Go to hell,' she said conversationally.

'I don't think you quite understand—'

The sound of a chair scraping the floor made parent and child spin around.

'No, it is you who do not understand. How long did you go away for the last time—five, out in two? I think you'll find that the law is less sympathetic to blackmail… With your record what are we talking, fifteen…?'

'Now, hold on, I came here to see my little girl,' he blustered.

Seb took a step closer, towering over the older man not just in his physical presence but his character. 'Not your little girl, *my* woman. You will empty your pockets, you will leave now and you will never come back. Believe me, you'll live to regret it if you don't.'

Looking visibly shaken, the older man began to back towards the door. Once there he raised his fist and shook it at them both. 'You'll be sorry when I sell my story.'

'I'm sorry.'

Seb turned, the pallor of her face causing him a spasm of alarm.

'What if he does?' she said, struggling to control the bubble of hysteria she could hear in her voice. 'The royal deal.'

'Forget him…' he roughed out. It was Mari he was worried about. 'Forget the bloody deal.'

She blinked, misunderstanding him. 'Of course, the dinner.' She took a deep breath. 'People will be arriving. We need to greet them. Don't worry, I won't let you down.'

'It doesn't matter…'

He was talking to air, as she had whisked out of the room and straight into the royal party.

Jaw clenched in frustration and left little choice, Seb painted on a social face and followed her.

Ironically, after dreading it Mari found herself dealing with the dinner without even a flicker of nerves, because she had bigger things to worry about now than using the wrong fork or forgetting the name of a famous guest.

She knew it was only delaying the inevitable, but as far as she was concerned it could go on forever. There was zero point pretending—she'd seen the seething contempt in Seb's eyes when he had given her father his marching orders. In Seb's eyes she was tainted. Where did that leave them?

Nowhere good.

The royal prince seated to her right said something and she smiled and nodded, not having a clue what he had said, but glad of the opportunity to look anywhere but at Seb. Normally at ease in any social situation—she had always envied him his poise—he had barely said a word to anyone all night.

'You are a lucky man, Seb.'

Seb tore his eyes from Mari and wondered why the hell it had seemed like a good idea to have her seated at the opposite side of the table. This damned meal was just going on and on forever.

'I know,' he said, thinking better late than never. Gutless, he thought in self-disgust. *I've been bloody gutless.* His way of dealing with his feelings for her, his solution, had been to quash them… *Gutless!*

'Give the chef my compliments.'

'Sure,' Seb returned as the waiter took away his untouched plate, cutting off for a moment his view of his wife. His wife sitting there looking poised as a queen while inside she must be… Pride and love welled up in his aching throat. While he was eaten up with shame that he'd not been able to protect her from the truth, at least he could protect her from anything that waste of space imagined he could do. The moment this damned thing was over he'd tell her.

It was not the only thing he planned to tell her.

'A toast to our lovely hostess.'

Seb, fighting a losing battle to control his impatience and frustration, closed his eyes and thought, *Not another one*!

Maybe he said it out loud, because the woman to his right laughed. Frankly he was past caring.

Her scattered wits were dragged back to the moment and the toast directed to her. Mari bowed her head in what she hoped passed for gracious thanks and…there was nothing, just a deep wrenching pain that made her cry out and bend forward, tumbling into blackness.

Mari heard voices but didn't open her eyes. Her head felt as though it were filled with cotton wool.

'Where am I?' She lifted a hand to her head and thought, *My God, I'm a walking, talking cliché.*

Except she wasn't walking; she was lying in bed. The sudden pain in her hand made her lower it; squinting at the drip brought the memory rushing back.

'The baby?'

Seb was there; maybe he'd been there all along. He didn't say anything; he didn't have to. It was there in his face.

'I'm so sorry.'

He took her hand, the one that didn't have the intravenous drip attached, and squeezed gently. She looked fragile enough to shatter, like a piece of semitransparent porcelain. 'It'll be fine.'

He clamped his jaw and swallowed the aching occlusion in his throat. It would be; it *had* to be.

For a time after the nightmare ambulance journey, when they had arrived at the hospital and he had been sidelined as the medical machine had swung into action, he had actually thought he had lost her.

The memory was enough to return the grey tinge to his skin. He braced his hand on the metal bed frame to stop it shaking as he fought his way clear of the expanse of aching empty darkness.

It was a place that he never wanted to visit again.

He never wanted to think of the precious moments they could have had, moments he had wasted because he had refused to accept that there were some things you could not control—like your heart.

Mari sighed and closed her eyes. When she woke Seb was still there, the shadow on his chin was darker and more pronounced and he was still wearing his dinner jacket.

'Why haven't you been home?' Then she remembered it wasn't her home and she wanted to cry. Instead she sniffed.

He smiled and looked beautiful and haggard as he caught her small hand between his. 'I didn't know what you'd get up to if I wasn't here.'

She struggled into a sitting position. 'I'm so sorry, Seb.'

'*You're* sorry?'

'Ruining your dinner. The baby, my father, everything, and don't worry, I know what you're going to say.'

He arched a dark brow and looked at her really strangely, but that might be the drugs they'd given her. She did feel a bit…floaty.

'You do?'

'Conman, jailbird father…' She forced back the rush of emotional tears that welled in her eyes by the sheer force of her will, and delivered in a carefully flat voice, 'No baby, the eighteen-month rule kicks in…' Her pale lips ghosted a smile. 'No-brainer?'

The smile just about broke his heart. With her hair pulled back by a nurse into a ponytail she looked so young, so fragile and so beautiful it hurt…*literally* hurt, a physical pain. Was this heartache? Before she came into his life he hadn't even acknowledged he had one; now he could barely think a sentence without referring to that organ!

'Get Sonia to pack my things. I'll go straight back to the flat,' she offered bravely.

'The hell you will!'

Her eyes widened; he wasn't being nice to her. 'I'll miss this,' she sighed.

'What?'

'You being a total jerk. Could you pass me

some water? I can…' Despite her protests, he held the glass to her lips.

He sat down beside her, making the mattress give. 'I think we should talk about it, don't you?'

She squeezed her eyes closed and shook her head. Talking about it was the last thing she wanted to do. Her baby was gone, and there was just a big black gaping hole.

'Look, I know you feel obliged not to throw me out because I've just come out of hospital, but I will be fine.'

'You're not fine.'

His loving tone brought tears to her eyes. 'And he'll do it, you know…my father, and it will be much easier for you to distance yourself from the scandal if I'm not here. In fact, if I'm not here there won't be a story.'

'I don't care about a story.'

'You do. My father is a criminal.'

'Yes, he is, which makes him very vulnerable to…*manipulation*.'

'I don't know what you mean.'

'I know, that's what I love about you, but let's just say that I have a feeling your father will be making a new life quite soon in Argentina.'

'He won't go.' But, God, she wanted him to. Did that make her a terrible person? Her own father…?

Seb gave a wolfish smile and kissed her. 'I can be very persuasive.'

'Well, even if he does go, I'm still his daughter, a bastard.' She lifted her teary eyes to his. 'I think our mother… I think she would have kept us if she could have, but he…'

'I think your mother wanted you to have a better life than she had.'

Mari nodded. 'And I have.'

He entwined his fingers in her small pale ones and lifted her hand to his lips, promising fervently, 'It's going to get even better, I promise.'

'There's no baby. You don't have to pretend.'

'The only thing I've pretended is that I didn't love you, but I do. You're my heart and soul, Mari.'

She looked up at him, wonder shining in her eyes like stars. 'You're not saying this because of the mi…mi…'

He squeezed her hand. 'Miscarriage.' He watched her wince and said calmly, 'We'll adopt. I've been thinking about it and you were right. Why bring a new baby into the world when there are so many children out there that need homes? We could adopt two, three if you like.'

'But you want a baby?'

He bent and kissed her lips with a tenderness that brought a fresh rush of hot, emotional tears to her eyes. 'I want you more. For a while back there…' His voice broke and with a groan he squeezed his eyes closed.

Mari watched, her heart thudding fast in her chest as he struggled for control, able to *feel* the intensity of his emotions. 'Seb…?' She stroked his hand.

At the light touch his eyes opened. 'Sorry, but…' He swallowed hard before continuing, 'You had lost a lot of blood, and I could never… I don't want to run the risk.' Fixed on her face now, his dark eyes held a shadow of the fear he had felt as he finished in a throaty whisper, 'I couldn't go through that again, Mari.'

She started to weep in earnest, great gulping sobs that shook her. 'You really love me?'

'I adore you.'

'But you were nice and polite to me.'

He burst out laughing. 'I promise I will never be polite to you again.'

She took his hand and lifted it to her lips, pressing a fervent kiss to his palm before spreading his long fingers around her cheek. 'I love you, Seb, so very much, but I can't stay married to you.'

Beneath his confident smile there was a hint of wariness as he asked, 'Why?'

'Because you're a Defoe and your name means a lot to you, you're proud of it and so you should be and I'm—'

'You're stupid,' he completed lovingly. 'I am proud. I'm proud of having the most beautiful woman in the universe as my wife.'

'I love you, Seb.'

'We have a lifetime to love. Right now you need to sleep.'

Mari struggled to keep her heavy eyes open. 'I can't, I want—'

'Don't worry, I'll be here when you wake up. I'll use the time to plan our wedding.'

Her tired eyes opened. 'We're already married.'

'I want to do it right this time... You deserve everything, my darling. A church, the dress, flowers, your foster dad to give you away. They were here, by the way, to see you, and Mark sends his love. Fleur is outside in the waiting room.'

'How about your parents?'

He shrugged. 'Why not? What is a wedding without a scandal? Though you do realise that no one will be looking at us with them there?'

Mari gave a watery smile; her eyes filled with tears that slid down her face. 'That would all be lovely,' she agreed. 'But all I really want, Seb, is you.'

He bent and pressed a long loving kiss to her pale lips. 'You've had me from the moment I saw you. I was just slow catching on.'

EPILOGUE

'LOOK AT YOUR SISTERS.'

Seb lifted his son, Ramon, up to see the babies sleeping side by side in the crib.

The toddler's eyes were wide.

'Can I touch?' he whispered.

Seb nodded, his heart swelling with pride as he watched his son touch a gentle finger to each baby's nose.

'They look like Mummy,' he said wonderingly as he stared at their golden-red curls.

'They do,' Seb agreed.

'Who do I look like, Daddy?'

Seb swallowed the lump of emotion in his throat. It was sometimes hard to believe how lucky he was. The early months of their marriage had been marvellous. After a fairy-tale wedding and extended honeymoon Mari had returned to her job at the school, which had accepted her back with open arms, scandal forgotten, after they realised she was married to the family who funded ten scholarship places.

But in the midst of their happiness, the shadow of the baby they'd lost had hung over them. It had been the arrival of Ramon, who had been one when they had adopted him, that had chased away the shadows, though not the precious memory of the baby they had lost.

He had been more terrified than he thought possible when Mari had fallen pregnant with twins. She, who had been working part-time since the adoption went through and with typical selflessness, had given up work immediately in an effort to ease his fears. If he hadn't had to keep it together for Ramon, Seb really thought he might have fallen apart. The little boy was a blessing in every way, and now they had two gorgeous daughters.

'You look like your birth mummy, Ramon, who loved you very much.'

'She went to live with the angels.'

'She did,' Seb agreed. 'Now, quiet, we don't want to wake the girls or Mummy, do we?'

Seb pressed a kiss to the forehead of his sleeping wife and left the room hand in hand with his son.

Outside, his brother-in-law, on the crutches he was due to exchange for a stick, stood waiting

with his wife—Mark had married his nurse—
and Fleur, who was talking to Mari's foster parents.

'You can go in,' Ramon told them all impor-
tantly. 'But only if you're very quiet—right,
Daddy?'

'Right.'

'And we're proud as Punch, aren't we?'

'We are,' Seb agreed, looking through the
window to where his wife slept. 'Very proud
and very, very lucky.'

* * * * *

LARGER-PRINT BOOKS!

GET 2 FREE LARGER-PRINT NOVELS PLUS
2 FREE GIFTS!

HARLEQUIN®

Romance

From the Heart, For the Heart

YES! Please send me 2 FREE LARGER-PRINT Harlequin® Romance novels and my 2 FREE gifts (gifts are worth about $10). After receiving them, if I don't wish to receive any more books, I can return the shipping statement marked "cancel." If I don't cancel, I will receive 4 brand-new novels every month and be billed just $5.09 per book in the U.S. or $5.49 per book in Canada. That's a savings of at least 15% off the cover price! It's quite a bargain! Shipping and handling is just 50¢ per book in the U.S. and 75¢ per book in Canada.* I understand that accepting the 2 free books and gifts places me under no obligation to buy anything. I can always return a shipment and cancel at any time. Even if I never buy another book, the two free books and gifts are mine to keep forever.

119/319 HDN GHWC

Name _____ (PLEASE PRINT)

Address _____ Apt. #

City _____ State/Prov. _____ Zip/Postal Code

Signature (if under 18, a parent or guardian must sign)

Mail to the **Reader Service:**
IN U.S.A.: P.O. Box 1867, Buffalo, NY 14240-1867
IN CANADA: P.O. Box 609, Fort Erie, Ontario L2A 5X3

Want to try two free books from another line?
Call 1-800-873-8635 or visit www.ReaderService.com.

* Terms and prices subject to change without notice. Prices do not include applicable taxes. Sales tax applicable in N.Y. Canadian residents will be charged applicable taxes. Offer not valid in Quebec. This offer is limited to one order per household. Not valid for current subscribers to Harlequin Romance Larger-Print books. All orders subject to credit approval. Credit or debit balances in a customer's account(s) may be offset by any other outstanding balance owed by or to the customer. Please allow 4 to 6 weeks for delivery. Offer available while quantities last.

Your Privacy—The Reader Service is committed to protecting your privacy. Our Privacy Policy is available online at www.ReaderService.com or upon request from the Reader Service.

We make a portion of our mailing list available to reputable third parties that offer products we believe may interest you. If you prefer that we not exchange your name with third parties, or if you wish to clarify or modify your communication preferences, please visit us at www.ReaderService.com/consumerchoice or write to us at Reader Service Preference Service, P.O. Box 9062, Buffalo, NY 14240-9062. Include your complete name and address.

HRLP15